KILL

THE

MALL

KILL

THE

MALL

PASHA MALLA

ALFRED A. KNOPF CANADA

PUBLISHED BY ALFRED A. KNOPF CANADA

Copyright © 2021 Pasha Malla

www.penguinrandomhouse.ca

Knopf Canada and colophon are registered trademarks.

Library and Archives Canada Cataloguing in Publication

Title: Kill the mall / Pasha Malla.
Names: Malla, Pasha, 1978- author.
Identifiers: Canadiana (print) 20190152672 | Canadiana (ebook) 20190152680 |
ISBN 9780735273498 (hardcover) | ISBN 9780735273504 (HTML)
Classification: LCC PS8626.A449 K55 2021 | DDC C813/.6—dc23

Text design: Lisa Jager
Cover design: Lisa Jager
Image credits: (mall) © Rashevskyi Viacheslav, Shutterstock.com;
(horse) © Grove Pashley, Getty Images

Printed and bound in Canada

2 4 6 8 9 7 5 3 1

Penguin
Random House
KNOPF CANADA

Sometimes you hear a xylophone
deep in the forest and you know
that things are just not right.

—JAMES TATE, *Memoir of the Hawk*

Let me be clear: I love the mall.

A mall's smell is a safe, sanitary one of judiciously filtered air and factory-fresh, unsullied clothing. It is the smell of nothing, yet nothing smells like a mall. The light is mild and even. There are no shadows in a mall. Its bathrooms are cleansed at regular intervals and verified on a timetable by diligent specialists. And food courts, which offer a bounty of choice to the hungry shopper, are the perfect place between purchases to grab some spaghetti or a submarine (sandwich), a cup o' soup or a lavishly buttered muffin. And then you station yourself amid the grid of symmetrical tables and devour whatever it is.

Malls often feature a central clock and/or fountain, an excellent location to stage a rendezvous. At every entrance colour-coded maps organize the stores by genre. Should you be perusing these maps, your own location is even revealed by a helpful "here's where you're now" icon. Not that getting lost in a mall should ever be traumatic, even to a child or foreigner. For how can you be lost anywhere so wonderful? It is fine advice, should you find yourself lost in a mall, to simply remain in place and wait for rescue.

It's true that in a mall you can be anyone, whether that's another body in a crowd or someone unusual balancing a bag of meat on his nose. Few locales provide such favourable circumstances to observe humanity and its various gaits. What joy it is to occupy a bench and view the crowds as a uniform mass heaving past like the unrelenting sea or time itself, or else to appreciate each person for his or her individuality: this one's legs are a little bandy, that one's eyes darting about with the virulence of a lunatic—what will she do, punch a cashier? Wait and see.

When the furor of it all proves too much, simply retreat to a change room. These are quiet, secluded places equipped with locks and mirrors for private self-evaluation. You try on a new outfit in there and turn one way, then the other, glimpsing yourself over your shoulder, and think: yes, perfect fit! And if not, many other clothing options are available, perhaps even the same garment in a more merciful size. You should never be ashamed of your body.

Malls are unparalleled for their accessibility. Frequently serviced by major bus routes, they also provide motorists ample parking in street-level lots, underground garages or multi-storey complexes with twisting driveways, like a roller coaster with less screaming—just don't forget your ticket, lest the mechanical arm trap you forever. Inside, a limited number of wheelchairs are available for provisional loan to the invalid and elderly.

Simply put, malls are where dreams come true. You enter with a notion of how the visit might transform your life, and re-emerge more pleased, and bettered, than you could have ever imagined. Salesclerks are great. For example, they are capable of producing a telescopic claw for fetching items from the higher shelves, or a ladder. Based on their training, they will offer counsel such as "Excellent choice, madam," or "I wouldn't dare if I were you, sir." And the selection! Unparalleled. In a mall, if you don't approve of the goods in one store, there's always another to cater to your tastes. On and on you go. And in the event that you can't find what you're after, some retailers will even permit special orders—a terrific excuse for a return trip.

All in all, I can think of no more civilized place on earth than a mall to shop, work and play. And now, by the divine miracle and generosity of your remarkable institution, for two months also to live. I truly hope that you will consider the enclosed application for this new residency program with as much thoroughness as I have expressed here re my feelings re malls. Which I, desperately, love.

Yours in trust,

ONE

THE REQUIREMENTS OF THE RESIDENCY were this: 50% of the time I was meant to be "engaging the public" and the other 50% "making work." Also, every week I was obliged to submit a Progress Report, culminating with a Final Report upon the termination of the residency, at which point the work I'd been making was also to be completed. How I was meant to be "engaging the public" was not specified. Nor was the type of "work" I was meant to be "making." And since I'd no idea how to go about "engaging the public" or "making work," it seemed impossible to gauge my progress, let alone craft reports on such a thing. How would it all end? In disgrace.

So on the first day of the residency a sort of pre-emptive humiliation tortured my spirits as I piloted my bicycle across town to the mall, which sprawled at the edge of the suburbs like the last standing outpost of some lost civilization. My application had been accepted via a simple one-page letter that outlined the preceding requirements and a date I was to show up and a date I was to leave. In addition to a small rucksack of clothing and hygiene equipment, this letter, tucked into my shirt pocket for safekeeping, was the only personal item I brought that morning. It was, after all, my ticket inside.

After chaining my bicycle to a conveniently located rack, I was greeted at the south entrance by the mall's caretaker, a woman named K. Sohail, per her nametag, who wore a beige uniform, a peaked cap, a monstrous ring of keys on her hip, and a perturbed expression, as if I'd interrupted something significant, or at least habitual. It suggested that my presence was, immediately, a nuisance. With an apologetic wince I pressed my Acceptance Letter to the glass and waited for K. Sohail to give it a once-over before she unlocked the door and permitted me inside.

Following a brisk, wordless handshake, with the squeak of her sneakers and the jingle of her keys echoing down the empty halls, K. Sohail led me to a store retrofitted with a small bathroom and a sleeping nook tucked behind a screen. She gestured vaguely toward a desk at which, I assumed, I was expected to produce the alleged work that would comprise 50% of my time; "engaging the public" would apparently happen out in the mall, among the masses.

Even in the abstract, "engaging the public" was a source of distress: I'm at my best at a remove, naturally more observer than mingler, and not much for small talk. Socially, I often sense that I'm disappointing people. But now, confronted with the very spaces in which I was meant to be fraternizing, the impending mortifications were all too vivid. I could think of nothing more dreadful than stalking the mall, arresting shoppers mid-purchase to engage in that brand of casual banter which, as I understood it, confers neither complete disinterest nor alarmingly intimate confession, but a generically moderate politesse that terrifies no one, and in fact somehow promotes camaraderie and goodwill. Such a thing requires an interpersonal dexterity, and perhaps personal dexterity as well, that, then as now, I've never been able to achieve. So I could predict the mall's patrons fleeing my "engagements" with disquiet—and possibly panic.

Acceptance Letter aside, it seemed unlikely that I was the right person for the job. In fact I could sense K. Sohail already sizing up my fraudulence, perhaps even forecasting the first travesty of a Progress Report she'd collect from me—and share in disbelief with her colleagues: *Behold this buffoon!* Did she have the power to terminate my residency? As always in moments of disgrace, in a sort of ingratiating mania I began to grovel. To not just acknowledge my inadequacies but to exploit them for pity.

I opened with some basic arithmetic.

Did the terms of the residency, I asked K. Sohail, not fail to account for time spent sleeping, eating and in the bathroom, activities that comprise about 40% of an average day, figuring eight hours for sleeping, an hour for eating and forty-five minutes for various ablutions and expulsions? Unless that 40% was meant to double as time spent "engaging the public"—if I was meant to be on display while, say, bathing—and "making work," whatever that might entail. But if not, the residency allotted only 60% of my time to divide between "engaging the public" and "making work," or 30%, then, each. Which was a far cry from the 50-50 split outlined in my Acceptance Letter, I told K. Sohail.

K. Sohail scratched her arm, glanced over her shoulder, straightened her belt.

Wasn't it, I continued, gesticulating madly, a concern that I would be spending more time performing unsanctioned activities than either of the two requirements of the residency? What if this sort of lawless behaviour were grounds for disqualification, I proposed to K. Sohail. It was an invitation to admit that the entire arrangement was a farce, but also an appeal to her humanity: No, I hoped she'd say, don't be silly, you'll be fine; you *are* fine.

Instead she showed me her watch.

The mall opened at nine.

It was quarter to.

Then, in what could have been an act of obligatory hospitality or a slyly cruel attempt at further humiliation, exposing me to every inch of the corridors that I would imminently debase, K. Sohail offered to let me tag along on her morning rounds.

What to do but obey?

Her sneakers proclaiming authority with each squeak, my own loafers pattering wretchedly behind, we passed shuttered shops yet to open for the day's trade: a jeweller; a plus-size clothier; a shoe store; a hairdresser replete with tri-colour pole. (Blood and bandages, I thought grimly.) In the centre of the mall was a handless clock that towered over a dried-up fountain; beyond it was the food court, but this we skirted to escalate to the mall's second level. At the top of the escalators was a vitrine dominated by sunflowers pressing their fat heads to the glass—like prisoners watching us pass.

K. Sohail took me down a narrow corridor to her office, a closet-sized room with a desk and a chair and a sink and some cleaning supplies, including a mop standing upright in its bucket, and an entire wall of closed-circuit TVs. On one of these TVs was the space assigned to me for the residency. The view scanned left to right and back again. I'd not noticed a camera previously. As I watched, the image crackled and fizzed. K. Sohail rapped the set with her knuckles. For a moment, a strange, weblike threading drizzled over the screen, as if a spider were casting its net over the camera lens. But then the picture jumped and cleared, and my living quarters returned, static and empty.

I sensed the caretaker waiting. The tour appeared to be wrapping up. Yet the way she lingered suggested that something remained unfinished. A formal expression of gratitude? A blood oath? Payment? I'd brought no cash, only plastic. Would she "take a card"?

But then a new horror dawned on me: what if the appropriate closure to the tour, with the two of us packed into that snug little room, bodies close, was a bout of lovemaking? Perhaps right there, on the floor of K. Sohail's office—"sealing the deal."

I turned from the monitors, dreading that I might discover K. Sohail unfolding a cot in the corner of the room, unbuckling her belt, preparing to have me.

But she was already gone, squeaking down the hall to the service elevator.

I joined her as the car arrived with a bang. Using a leather strap, she hauled open the doors, which parted top to bottom like a mandible. In we climbed and descended. I noticed, apart from two buttons conventionally marked 2 (for the second floor) and G (for ground), a third button with no corresponding symbol, blank as a lozenge stuck to the steel panelling. Before I could ask K. Sohail where it led, she was heaving open the doors and leading me past a room heaped with garbage into the main thoroughfare, where the first few patrons were filtering in from outside.

The mall was open for business.

My residency had begun.

QUICKLY IT BECAME CLEAR that this was not a top-notch mall.

The hour crept past ten and still most, if not all, of the stores remained unopened, with their security doors bracketed in place and the lights off inside. Their names, decalled or embossed above the doorways—Sugarhut, Hap 'n' Stance, Pet Realm—seemed to refer to enterprises long bankrupted or abandoned, empty save a few barren shelves and skeletal display racks. Also, most of what I had assumed to be customers were in fact people using the mall as an air-conditioned thoroughfare to locales beyond. From my quarters I watched them pass without so much as a glimpse at me and what I was (or wasn't) doing, moving with the focused transience of people with other places to be; their minds, I sensed, were already there.

That said, this obliviousness was preferable to someone actually stopping outside the residency space to have a look, zoologically, at me. When this did finally happen, I began to shuffle my materials around as if I'd been caught in an organizational interlude. Even so, this spectator, a woman in an ornate, luridly floral hat, kept peering in—watching me with, I assumed, expectations. So I shuffled things around some more, wondering how long I would have to maintain this ruse before "getting back to work" when I'd never been working in the first place. (What would that entail? A dance?)

At last the ornately hatted woman gave up and moved on, but not before I heard her sigh. In disappointment, I imagined. Or perhaps pity.

For lack of any other purpose or function, I decided to write down this episode: my first experience "engaging the public," as it were. I became so invested in chronicling what had happened that I failed to notice that the ornately hatted woman had returned. When I looked up she was watching me again, but now with something like intrigue. Hunched over the table, scribbling away, I likely appeared to be "making work." I acknowledged her with a curt nod and then returned to this supposed work, one eyebrow cocked to convey diligence and focus as my pen flew over the page.

After a while—satisfied, presumably—the woman left. I sat back from the desk, my hand cramping faintly, and turned the episode over in my mind. Not only had I staged a tantalizing performance for which a patron had returned for an encore, I had also fulfilled both requirements of the residency: "engaging the public" (the ornately hatted woman's rapturous spectatorship) and "making work" (writing up the episode). Then a revelation struck. I had in fact, to borrow an old idiom, killed three birds with one shrewdly hurled stone—for what was the document sitting before me but the beginning of a possible Progress Report? With a slash of my pen, the episode with the ornately hatted woman became The Episode with the Ornately Hatted Woman, transmuted from a faintly mortifying occurrence into a document of the very same. I was awed by my own ruthless efficiency and tact: my Progress Reports could double as my "work"!

By then it was lunchtime and, as you can imagine, I'd worked up quite an appetite.

I left my quarters and headed over to the food court, where, my Acceptance Letter claimed, I would be entitled to three meals a day, free of charge, as a condition of the residency. Unfortunately the only open restaurant, or food stall, was one staffed by a team of teenagers roasting chickens. In an electrified wall-oven, rows of the things twirled sluggishly, sizzling and brown and lacquered with grease. One, please, I ordered from the teens, and a chicken was liberated and hacked into portions and presented upon a mattress of shredded leaves. To drink: iced tea.

The food court was a cavernous facility with a cathedral ceiling that culminated in a domed skylight, though what sunshine it permitted was subsumed by the mall's yellow drone of phosphorescence. I occupied a table a dozen or so spaces over from the only other diners, a man and woman who sat side by side (an arrangement I interpreted as marital) to share their box of chicken. I sawed away at the bird's hindquarters until I'd dispatched a flap of meat onto my plastic fork, but before I could make my first sampling a low gurgling sound interrupted me from the neighbouring table.

As I watched, the husband fell from his chair, clutching his throat, and hit the floor like a swatted insect. His wife launched atop him and began pummelling his chest with her fists. This continued for some time until he produced a fierce retching noise and rocketed upright. Something sprung from his lips and traced a perfect arc, glinting in the food court's subdued lighting, before landing beside my foot.

A ring, slathered with drool and crafted in gold.

I held it up and asked the couple if it was theirs. The wife, hauling her husband to his feet, shook her head.

I wiped the ring on my napkin and, with the white paper providing an agreeable backdrop, gave it a better look. The edges were slightly bevelled, and a crease running along the middle sectioned it into two hemispheres. But, wait, no—not a crease. A single black hair, coiled around the ring. This I pulled free and, after some struggles—it clung soggily to my finger—flicked away.

The ring looked more pleasing now, less complex. I tried it on: a perfect fit. Turning my hand over, back and then front, I admired its appearance on my hand. Elegant. I glanced up and the couple was gone—or, rather, at one of the garbage depositories at the edge of the food court, sliding the ruins of their lunch into the netherworld beyond. Fair enough. Had I vomited a ring, I wouldn't feel like chicken either.

But here I wondered, too, if I shouldn't feel guiltier about profiting from a stranger's folly. Did this count as "engaging the public"? The ring suddenly felt oppressive and unearned. I slid it free for another, more scrupulous review. Something, I discovered, had been etched inside the band. Perhaps a name or dedication? I brought the ring to the tip of my nose and angled it to the light to pick out the inscription . . .

There it was: *Now*, engraved in a calligraphic script. More words followed. I squinted, turning the ring slowly. What followed was a full phrase, its final period like a door closing upon the sentence—yet somehow also opening to new possibilities.

Now, said the ring, *you are mine.*

MY FIRST NIGHT IN THE MALL was solitary. Well, they were all solitary, but that initial experience of the lights dimming as the halls emptied, and the few open shops shuttering for the day, and the teens at the chicken restaurant clearing out on wafts of grease was one of abandonment. Not that I'd entertained any patrons apart from the ornately hatted woman, or spoken to anyone other than K. Sohail and the chicken-roasting teens. The closest operational enterprise to my quarters was the hairdresser, which existed only as a faintly septic odour of permanent solution drifting down the hall, and I'd seen no evidence of life from it all day.

Still, as the mall shut down for the night I was overwhelmed by a sudden, desperate solitude deeper than any I'd ever known. Not simply an awareness that I would be spending the night deserted in the mall—but that I was alone in the universe. What a lonely fleck of nothing I was, I thought, amid it all, with only the slight hiss of the air ducts for company. The bluish glow of the mall's security lighting felt subaquatic, making me little more than some prehistoric plankton fossilized and forgotten in the ocean floor.

Sitting there at my workstation before a draft of my first Progress Report, which I'd spent most of the afternoon revising and now seemed pathetic and vain, I removed from my pocket the ring I'd found at lunch. At first the inscription had felt invasive. But now, in this total isolation, being told *you are mine* acknowledged me as a person, albeit proprietarily. So I slid the ring back onto my finger. It really was a splendid fit—remarkable how natural it looked on my hand, as if crafted just for me.

Wearing it, too, secreted the inscription: now *it* was *mine*—and not, as the writing claimed, that I was somehow its. But then this provoked worry: What if the ring passed from my possession? What if, say, K. Sohail claimed it as lost property with ambitions of restoring it to its rightful owner? Would some part of me abscond with it? My soul, say—or my sanity? If the ring and I now belonged to each other, I could never take it off.

These thoughts were interrupted by the beam of a flashlight swinging out of the dark. The caretaker herself! I cowered, anticipating a reprimand or gunfire, and hid my ringed finger beneath the table. But K. Sohail, preceded by squeaks and jingles, was simply on her nightly surveillance circuit of the mall. Pausing before my quarters she asked if I required anything—I said no—and then, shockingly, in a sudden, almost violent gesture she unfolded a slatted barricade from one side of my quarters to the other, and locked it up. Caging me within like a beast, or a jailbird!

Yet here she paused again. Silence, bloated with anticipation, hung between us. Her body a silhouette on the other side of the grating, wavering slightly. Mine at my workstation. That strange blue light glowing all around. And then, as if to temper the insult of my imprisonment, she leaned forward and whispered through the slats: *Goodnight*.

Listening to K. Sohail squeak and jingle off into the mall, and presumably onward to her home—jingle-squeaking across town to her front door, to her fridge for a slurp of juice, to the bathroom and finally to bed—I found my thoughts consumed less with the locked grate (basic protocol, I assumed—after all, who was I to freely wander the mall without supervision?) than wonder: had there been something tender, and not just perfunctory or required, in K. Sohail's parting words? (or word?)

How sad it is to wish another person goodnight! A gentle nudge into the unknown, so much more forlorn than goodbye. *Goodnight* implies not just physical but spiritual departure—to sleep, the ultimate solitude. Even for those lucky enough to share beds with a loved one, the nighttime voyages of the mind remain private; we return with no souvenirs, no means to capture where and who we've been—and few things are more futile than a retold dream.

Goodnight, K. Sohail, I thought.

Is there anything so lonely as it is to fall asleep?

THE FOLLOWING MORNING I settled into the schedule I kept for most of the residency: wake as K. Sohail arrived to open the mall (and my quarters) around 8:30, perform my morning ablutions and proceed to the food court for a breakfast of eggs and tea. Back at my desk, I would spend the morning honing my Progress Report until noon, when I returned to the food court for lunch (chicken, iced tea), before putting in an afternoon of further "work." Then, dinner (lunch leftovers, sparing me another visit to the food court), the mall would shut down, and after a period of staring longingly into the dark, waiting for K. Sohail's good-night—swiftly deployed, yet dancing at the edge of something profound and thrilling.

Amid this routine, over those first seven days occurred a few moments of note.

On the fifth day of my residency, I met K. Sohail on my way back from lunch. She had a garbage bag stuffed to the gills slung over each shoulder, and when I asked her what she was carrying, she told me, without breaking stride: hair. And then she was gone, squeaking and jingling off into the recesses of the mall.

Hair from the hairdresser, I assumed. But that didn't add up: not once on my trips to and from the food court had I noticed a single customer having their hair cut. Nor, from my quarters only two shops over, had I ever overheard the telltale snip of scissors or buzz of electric shears. Nor had I witnessed anyone passing through the mall with a freshly coiffed "do" or a salon-slick pomade. The only sign of life in the hairdresser's was, in fact, the hairdresser herself, sitting in the back of the shop with her face hidden by a magazine—and even then she was motionless; the pages didn't turn.

Sure enough, as I rounded the corner past the defunct clock and parched fountain and stole a quick glance around the twirling barber's pole, there the hairdresser sat, still as a pillar behind her magazine, with no sign of customers or any evidence of a recent haircut having taken place. As always, the hairdresser was utterly alone, her scissors and combs stolidly at rest in their jars of blue juice. The scene could have been a photograph—no, a painting: not a scene excerpted from life, but an image plucked from the imagination without context or concern for what might precede or follow it.

So where did all that hair come from?

Back in my quarters, pen poised above the page, I turned the episode over in my mind. Was the mystery of the bags of hair entrancing enough to demand documentation? Though the whole thing was curious, it inspired only questions, and a Progress Report was intended for answers, declarations, the supremacy of facts. Besides, it felt wrong to implicate K. Sohail in my reports, since she was the one collecting them. Acknowledging her role felt indecent, like turning the camera around onto the cinematographer, or fleeing the country in a lover's pants.

So I left the episode undocumented—for now.

The next day, on my post-lunch digestive walk—worrying faintly that, save the Episode with the Ornately Hatted Woman, I'd accrued no additional public engagements worth mentioning in my first Progress Report, which was starting to feel a little thin, no matter how many times I revised it—I discovered that the halls of the mall were totally empty. The crowds had been thinning all week and now even the occasional stragglers had vanished: if they had been in transit to locales beyond, perhaps they'd all arrived and were now happily ensconced wherever that was.

Having completed a circuit of the lower level, I circled back to the food court and the base of the escalators. They seemed so ghostly: one set lifted emptily and endlessly to the second floor, while the other cycled its vacant steps back down.

Up I went, and shortly found myself before the sunflower display I'd first encountered on K. Sohail's introductory tour. Remarkably, the store was open. Whether whoever staffed the sunflower store (a sunflorist?) might count as "the public" or not, I was starting to feel a little desperate. All week all I'd done was edit the same Progress Report, and the effect of each subsequent revision was to eradicate the actual Episode. The document wasn't just thin, it now read like a fabrication, and the person in it, the one who "worked" while the ornately hatted woman observed, had ceased to be me at all, but a *character*. K. Sohail was due to collect it the following day!

So I decided to introduce myself to one of the mall's scant proprietors.

The sunflower store, it turned out, was actually a wholesaler of household decorations; its name was Kookaburra. A riot of knickknacks and curios and tchotchkes were piled on shelves or stacked in displays around the packed showroom floor. Sunflowers did feature heavily, painted upon the faces of clocks or patterned upon wallpaper or sculpted in copper on the handles of dessert spoons, and a great jungle of the things spilled from the vitrine into the store. Some of these towered over eight feet tall, their monstrous heads lolling up near the ceiling—stooping, it seemed, to inspect me as I crept beneath. I assumed that they were artificial, as none were potted and their stalks appeared to be fixed to the floor, but I didn't dare touch even the smallest plant to confirm it.

Despite the ubiquitous bric-a-brac, one thing Kookaburra did not have was an employee. No one worked the counter or prowled the aisles or arranged the displays or pruned the sunflowers, and when I rang the little bell by the cash register, not a soul appeared. So I went over to the doorway marked Kooks Only, poked my head inside and, with uncharacteristic brazenness, announced myself to the shadows.

Waited. Listened.

No reply.

And then, on a faint gust of wind—from the ventilation ducts?—a loose tumbleweed of hair came spinning out of the dark, right up to my foot, and snagged on my shoe. I reached down to remove it. How coarse the thing was, like the bundled wire of a scouring pad. My hand retracted in revulsion. Instead of pulling it free, I wiped my foot on a nearby birdbath, though the hairball took several vigorous scrapings to dislodge, clinging to my loafer like a clot of burrs. Stranger still, that wiry little nest appeared to seethe for a moment before it caught another draft and went scuttling back down the hall.

PROGRESS REPORT #1

What is more edifying than the admiration of another human being? To be liked, or even loved, is why we exist. Every morning upon waking we wonder, "Whom shall I persuade to like me today?" Of course affection takes many forms, be it a subtle nod of approval—*excellent work, continue*—or a juicy smooch on the mouth accompanied by sensual fondling, or a father's preference for the sturdiest of his sons. Whatever your pleasure, it's likely the pleasure of other people's pleasure in you.

Say for example you are working—diligently, of course, for at least 30% of your waking hours, and perhaps even more—and a stranger comes strolling by. The sheer fervour of your dedication stops her dead in her tracks. "This one is taking his role seriously," she thinks, reeling in awe. "He is a contributor and not a leech slurping from the open vein of society. I simply must pause to enjoy this moment, hat-fitting appointment be damned!"

Work is the lifeblood of humanity. But love is the lifebones (equally essential). For blood without a form is just a red mess on the floor. Also important are skin and musculature—food and water, in this analogy—and a nervous system/brain, which we might equate to, for example, engaging the public. For what is society without socializing? Nothing. Or maybe something else with another, lonelier name. It's simply that powerful.

And what better way to engage the public than with one's work? It comes full circle, like a snake eating itself to death. You make work, you engage the public, and love erupts like a volcano or a boil. Work, engage, love . . . work, engage, love . . . and so on, the basic recipe by which the greatest civilizations have thrived throughout history. The worst civilizations having employed a different, useless recipe, so theirs are now the ruins we plunder for gold.

In conclusion, 60% of the day spent making work and engaging the public almost isn't enough! Because every wave of adoration that crashes over you is like a drug that whips you into a frenzy for more. I'll say it again: love is a drug, and so is work. And what an inspiration that each member of the public, or a colleague, might love you for your zeal for work and catch the addiction, and return to her own work with renewed passion, burning with the fervent hope that someone will end up loving her, too.

MIDWAY THROUGH THE SECOND WEEK of my residency I decided to get a haircut. Or, more honestly, the conditions of my hair forced me to act. I am not usually one to trust any part of my body, even its dead cells, to a stranger. However, the tufts around my ears had gotten so wild and feathery that at night they tickled and kept me awake. So off to the salon I went, hoping, at the very least, for access to a scissors—even if I had to deploy the device myself.

Again I encountered an empty room save the woman at the back with her face buried in a magazine. Tentatively I made my approach, halting a few paces away in the middle of the shop. Cleared my throat. Introduced myself as the person residing a few doors over, outlined the 50-50 work/public engagement balance, offered a quick equivocation about the actual arithmetic per sleep/ablutions/etc., and made my request: Just a quick trim, if you please.

No reply.

The magazine didn't budge; no grateful or curious or livid face emerged.

I tried again. A simple enough thing to ask. And while I would never describe myself as a master of social decorum, I was certain that asking for a haircut in an establishment that specialized in said enterprise wasn't outlandish or vulgar. In fact, I felt like I was acting conventionally—even reasonably.

Still nothing. The woman didn't even flinch.

But then I wondered if perhaps I was overstating the obvious. If *asking* for a haircut in a salon was, in fact, egregious. Of course that's why I was here! What a fool I was to explain myself. So, amid burning shame, I assumed one of the expressly designed chairs and waited to be tended, avoiding my own eyes in the mirror and instead gazing down at the tiles. The pattern, the pale colour, their stark sterility—the things seemed to swim up off the floor, the lines between them deepening, turning cavernous, plummeting down as each tile seemed to float up and lift . . .

I felt myself in a sort of swoon, unable to look away . . .

Lines blurred . . . The air turned liquid . . . I felt myself swimming in it . . . Or drowning . . .

And everything faded.

Some time passed. I'm not sure how much. Apparently I slept, or passed out. Because the floor—previously spotless—was now covered with what was unmistakably my hair. Same colour, same consistency, yet now disengaged from my scalp and orphaned upon the tiles. I had no memory of a cut. But a glimpse in the mirror confirmed it: I'd been treated to a neat and tidy trim. Perhaps a little shorter than I would have preferred, but a decent haircut all the same.

Bewildered, I looked to the back of the shop. There the alleged hairdresser sat, motionless, with the magazine blocking her face.

I offered thanks. Again she didn't budge or acknowledge me. Had I enraged her? Perhaps falling asleep during a haircut was another breach of etiquette. Fearing that I'd humiliated myself yet again, from a wall-chart of prices I situated myself accordingly, swiped my credit card through the device beside the cash register, and without another word slunk back to my quarters—where, I discovered, nearly *three hours* had passed.

Then the itching began.

First it was my neck. Prickling and needling, like being strangled by a cactus. Assuming clippings were trapped in my shirt, I pried open my collar. But as I did so the itch scurried down between my shoulder blades. And no sooner were my fingernails clawing at *that* spot, an area further down inflamed. It was infuriating: every place I scratched only seemed to chase the feeling elsewhere. There was no recourse but to bathe—for a second time that day, no less. The inefficiency rankled me. But these circumstances were extreme.

I ducked behind the screen, out of view of the cameras, removed my clothing, wrapped my lower half in a towel and entered the bathroom. As water thundered into the tub, I stood at the sink eyeing my new hairstyle in the mirror, clipped so close at the temples that my skin shone palely through. In addition to the cuttings that my shirt had trapped all over my torso, stubble had also collected on my cheeks and in my ears. I brushed as much as I could into the sink, where it collected in a bristly spackle.

But now that itch had found its way into my mouth.

After gargling with water the feeling remained, so I moved close to the mirror and opened wide. There it was, a stout hair perched almost defiantly on the middle of my tongue. Except my attempts to wipe it away did nothing, and when I took it between my thumb and forefinger and pulled, it held fast. The hair, about the thickness and length of an eyelash, was somehow attached.

I got a better grip with my fingernails and tried again: like a follicle, a taste bud lifted with it. But the hair didn't loosen. In fact it seemed to grip with renewed purpose—not simply affixed to the surface of my tongue but somehow lodged into the deeper tissue. Surely, I thought with horror, it couldn't be growing there? I shuddered, collected myself, opened my mouth again, pinched the hair at the tip and yanked sharply. Something gave and snapped, like a blade of grass plucked from the earth by its root. But to my horror the hair did not pop free. Instead it began unravelling.

What protruded from my tongue, it seemed, was merely the tip of something much longer. I pulled and pulled, as if reeling in a fishing line, and out it came: an inch turned into another, and then another. Worse still was the tugging sensation of the hair slipping along inside my tongue. Watching myself in the mirror, eyes wide in horror, though my instinct was just to rip the thing free, I proceeded gently so as not to break it off. A foot of the stuff, then two, gathering in the sink in coils. With the bath still running the bathroom was filling with steam; my reflection fogged over. Lost in mist, I groped wildly at my mouth—and still the hair unravelled, thickening from thread to string, braided and bristly and slimy, and slithering still out of a widening hole in my tongue. Relentless. Seemingly without end.

So I closed my lips, pressed my teeth around that cord of hair, and began to chew.

THOUGH THE EPISODE with the really long hair growing from my tongue was easily the most notable occurrence of my residency so far, it felt too grotesque to document in a Progress Report. Besides, it wasn't an example of "engaging the public" at all, but something private and harrowing. And though I'd been able to bite it off at the root, a little bristle of hair remained, troubling my palate when I closed my mouth. More disturbing was the sense that this was only "the iceberg's tip," and that far more hair threaded inside my tongue, down my throat into a nest in my chest, from which tendrils trailed along my arms and legs into my hands and feet—hair like veins through my flesh, coursing under the skin.

Which is to say that the episode wasn't yet over.

Sitting at my desk that evening, the empty page of my alleged second Progress Report before me, mind wandering, I became fixated on the video camera scanning the room. An eye, watching me. Seeking. But whose eye? K. Sohail's? No, she was merely a technician, beholden to the same shadow organization that administered my residency; her goodnights suggested the subdued camaraderie of diminished souls. Yet we weren't quite allies, either. Perhaps because of my limited tenure at the mall, K. Sohail seemed to be keeping her distance. She had bigger fish to fry, as the saying went, than the puny minnow of me.

Watching the camera blink and scan, I thought about how each Progress Report was meant to document my residency— "making work," that is, as well as "engaging the public." But how could they compete with actual footage? Considering the ubiquity of surveillance throughout the mall, all that video evidence surely better captured my day-to-day than a few futile paragraphs. If a picture was indeed worth a thousand words, at twenty-four frames per second those cameras were producing an alarming 1,440,000 words *every minute*. How could writing compete?

Perhaps, I thought, my Progress Reports should be less dedicated to documentation than to impressions. After all, I needn't confess every gory detail of my existence, but merely offer something that the videos could not. So why not put pen to paper to recast the Episode of the Haircut and the Subsequent, Possibly Related Episode of the Really Long Hair Growing from My Tongue such that its disturbing reality might—why not?—turn jovial on the page. And perhaps, refashioned as entertainment, the resulting version might even soften the trauma of the real thing.

A fine idea, but, in practice, with the camera rotating back and forth above me, dramatizing the haircut proved hopeless. It wasn't simply a matter of mysteriously occluded events (I had, of course, had haircuts before that were easy enough to recollect); each word seemed utterly detached from even my imagined reconstruction of the episode. *Scissors* offered a vague stencil of an object that had nothing to do with the tremulous sensation of blades snicking past one's earlobe. And not only that, but the Progress Report relied on the blunt stakes of language to pin down the shifting nebulae of sensation and sentiment: hard enough to itinerate, trickier still to concoct.

The problem was the gap: what had transpired during my blackout? There had been no hair growing from my tongue before the haircut; now there was one, indeed. I needed to watch those tapes. Partly to see what I was missing, but also to mitigate what was becoming an existential crisis. And maybe the camera might reveal not just what had happened but, via its detached perspective, some personal truth to which I was ignorant, and which I might harness in my reports—and maybe even in my life.

Yet I couldn't bring myself to ask K. Sohail for access to the footage. Beyond her goodnights, the one time that I'd encountered her out in the mall, lugging those bags of hair, she'd seemed flustered. The meeting had been out of context, a disruption of her routine—and I of all people appreciate the sanctity of habit. I also sensed that I existed to her as something of a burden, and there was an undeniable element of distrust in the fact that, despite her goodnights, she modified my quarters into a cell every night. (Which, again, I appreciated: the mall was her responsibility, and hers alone, and each night she left it unattended to a stranger whose only credentials were a one-page letter claiming a right to be there.)

Since I was never alone in the mall with free access to roam about, unmonitored, the solution seemed to be taking advantage of K. Sohail's morning rounds, that brief window during which my quarters were unlocked and she wasn't yet in her office. Only then might I sneak up to the second floor for a quick look at the tapes. Nothing too nefarious. Were there not in fact cultures that believed the camera performed a sort of thievery of the soul? My plan was to simply reclaim it. In this way, I fancied myself something of a maverick.

I lay in bed the following morning, waiting for K. Sohail to come jingling and squeaking down the hallway. When she at last approached—right on cue—I made sure to lean out from behind the screen, as I did every morning, and wave as she unlocked and folded back the gate.

She nodded in reply, then headed off to the service elevator. Immediately I stole from my bed, grabbing only my credit card (for lock-picking purposes), and, in stockinged feet and nightwear, hightailed it in the opposite direction to the escalator. I bolted up to the second floor, ducked past the sunflowers and, peeking through the little window hatched with wire, watched K. Sohail unlock and enter her office and pause before that wall of screens.

I hadn't considered two things: one, that the cameras might not, in fact, be "live," but instead relay their footage through some sort of retrospective delay, such that K. Sohail would witness me scampering through the mall, and the gig (jig?) would be, as they say, up. And what then? Arrest? Some sort of psychosexual flogging? Dismissal from my residency, surely, at the least.

But there, on the screen that displayed my quarters, nothing was amiss. I might well have still been in bed behind the screen.

Except! What if each morning K. Sohail stood, just as she did now, watching her monitors and in fact *waiting for me* to make my way to the food court for breakfast before she commenced her rounds? Meaning that when I didn't emerge as usual, she'd realize that some malfeasance was afoot. Might she then go down to check on me, and upon finding my bed and bathroom empty realize that I'd snuck off?

My breath caught in my throat. My scheme was ill planned. Who was I to try to outfox the mall?

Well, I fled—down the hall, searching desperately for an open store in which to hide.

While Kookaburra was, today, closed, a few shops down I discovered the House of Blues, a new operation specializing in denim products, open for business. As I entered, a young man came bounding at me from behind the cash register, eyes aflame with, I assumed, the prospect of a potential commission.

The salesman told me his name (Dennis), that it was "opening day," and—sincerely, I think—that he would be happy to assist me however he was able. (From his lingering glance at my pyjamas, I sensed he already had ideas.)

Dennis was twentyish, luxuriantly ponytailed and dressed in an entire outfit crafted from the finest marbled denim: an open jean jacket revealed a matching shirt beneath, which in turn bled into a pair of identical trousers; even his shoes, which boasted little denim tassels that flickered insouciantly with his every step, synchronized with the rest of his ensemble. He was, without question, a remarkable specimen, right on the cutting edge of the latest fashions and full of that guileless abandon particular to youth.

Concerned that my naturally dour and somewhat furtive demeanour might ruin "opening day," I looked away in shame and propriety—right into the glaring eye of a security camera.

I wheeled back to him with renewed vigour: Wonderful, Dennis, I am here to buy some new pants!

Well, Dennis set to it like a creature possessed. In a delirium he tore jeans from displays and unclipped jeans from racks and even removed jeans from mannequins, knocking them to the floor and wrenching the pants from their lower halves.

Though my request had been merely a tactic of subterfuge, I was quickly swept away upon the tide of Dennis's passion. As he collected armloads of jeans, I found myself *actually wanting* pants now. Would he prove a genius of intuition, and find me "just the thing"? Would we metaphysically commune, via jeans?

More honestly, I wanted to impress Dennis. Don't we all long to inspire a shopkeeper's awe at our fluency with their wares? *Wow, yes, we want the salesperson to marvel. From all these selections—you've done even better than I'd imagined.* In a way, you've set them free.

We were both really in the thick of it now!

What an "opening day" this was going to be for Dennis, who now, ponytail swaying, climbed a ladder to fetch his most rarefied merchandise from the highest shelves. Denim in all the colours of the oceans—blues, of course, but also greys and greens and blacks as profound as the bowels of the earth—came cascading down from the ceiling and settled on the floor of the House of Blues. And the styles! Shredded to rags, tight as suction, baggy enough to permit room for two. Just as it was all beginning to feel hopeless— how to choose from all this choice?—my heart leapt to my throat. In a strangled voice I cried out: Wait!

Dennis paused. Teetering slightly on the ladder, he turned to spread his most recent selection like a set of denim angel's wings. *These?*

I held my breath, examining the jeans in their full glory. A strategic distress of the fabric, a gentle taper, a set of pleats as subtle as the windswept sands, and a single, tantalizing "rock and roll" slash across the left knee. Extraordinary. But were they the ones for me? I met Dennis's eyes. There was something in them, something imploring: like a true master, he wouldn't guide me patronizingly through to the other side, only lead me to the edge of revelation. And here was my moment . . .

I nodded. Those, I told him, please.

To my relief, Dennis nodded back. Scrambled down from his perch, grinning the whole way. Once he was back on solid ground, in a gesture of surprising paternity he clasped my shoulder with one hand and pressed the jeans into my arms with the other.

I took them. They were so soft—yet durable, too. A jean one could trust.

Dennis grinned, patted me on the upper arm, and retreated behind the till to ring up my purchase.

I produced my credit card from the pocket of my pyjamas.

I awaited more than the imminent swipe.

And here it was, delivered with a cockeyed glance and an awestruck shake of the head: Excellent choice.

Excellent choice!

By god, I'd done it. The jeans, and Dennis's veneration, were mine.

A COMRADE IN THE MALL presented thrilling possibilities.

In a hospitable turn of seniority, I invited Dennis to join me for lunch, at which I suggested we split a chicken—"on me"—though our iced teas would remain independent ventures. New to the mall, Dennis was undeniably impressed at my expertise in navigating the food court. Assuming my regular table, I explained to him that this location was ideal since it was out of smell range of both the washrooms and the garbage area, concealed by the escalator from the purview of the chicken teens, and also positioned with a scenic view of the skylight and the sunshine beyond.

I sawed the chicken in half, placed Dennis's portion on a mat of napkins and mentored him briefly on strategies to liberate meat from bone. The conversation that accompanied our meal was scant—check-ins as to each other's satisfaction with the food; admiration of my new jeans, which I'd donned overtop of my pyjamas; a fleeting, mostly benign argument over who would dispose of the skeleton once we'd picked the bird clean—yet felt tinged with melancholy. Surely Dennis noted the dearth of patrons in the mall, and what this entailed for the viability of his House of Blues. Since I didn't dare broach his shop's imminent failure and the dashing of his dreams upon the rocks of bankruptcy, instead I offered to refill his iced tea; he declined.

Those simple words—No, thank you—seemed to echo out from our table and to swell up to the heights of the food court's ceiling, pressing against the skylight as though trapped and trying to escape; then, defeated, withering back down and dispersing like some noxious gas, rolling out from the food court and down the empty hallways of the mall, all the way to my quarters, where my desk and bed were finally swallowed in a fog of annihilation . . . I shook the image free from my thoughts and returned my attention to Dennis, who, ponytail lolling over his shoulder, was pensively chewing his chicken. Had he been picturing the same scenario?

What I'd hoped from this new-found companionship, initiated in the House of Blues and now sanctified with our first lunch together, was that, as it had during our earlier transaction, Dennis's youthful exuberance might jubilate my own depleted spirits. Instead, watching Dennis dislocate the chicken's leg to gnaw some purple meat from the gleaming joint, I sensed the sorrow of the mall infecting him. I ought to say something encouraging, I thought, something to convey hope and possibility— although perhaps solidarity awaited us at the nadir of Dennis's plummeting spirits, rather than through me, falsely buoying him aloft from below.

Yes, Dennis and I had shared the bliss of commerce, the sure inauguration of a lifelong fraternity. Yet there were truths about the mall that he would have to glean on his own. It was still too early, for example, to announce that a hair growing out of my tongue might be colonizing the rest of my body. Nor could I trouble him with my worries about the ubiquitous surveillance in the mall, what the footage might be used for, who was monitoring it—and why. And certainly I couldn't detail the complexities of my relationship with K. Sohail, viz. the tantalizing tension between the officious way she imprisoned me and her gentle and, dare I say, almost fond goodnights.

No, this was only our first chicken. Soon enough the mall would deflate Dennis's spirits until we were equally bereft. Only then could we freely commune—about the mall, about our potentially shared purpose in it, about what we might accomplish together amid such overwhelming desolation. For now, after I'd pitched the ruins of our lunch into the garbage, all we could do was shake hands, thank each other for a swell morning, and head our separate ways "back to work," such as it was: Dennis up the escalator to the House of Blues, and I to my quarters, where the week's Progress Report still remained a blank page on my desk—and in my mind.

THE HAIR WAS GROWING.

Fortunately I'd brought a razor, and one morning toward the end of my second week, driven to distraction all night by that horrible tickle against the roof of my mouth, I rocketed from bed straight to the mirror, lathered my tongue with cream, and set to carefully shaving. This task I performed not without shame, and although I'd successfully hacked the protuberance to a speck amid the pink flesh, at lunch I ate my chicken with a hand over my mouth, lest Dennis glimpse the freakish horror therein.

Our relationship was progressing nicely; two days in I already sensed in my new friend a growing despair. He wondered aloud where all the people were, and I consoled him that they seemed to come in waves, recalling my first day in the mall, when a relative mob descended from the main entrance—though I refrained from mentioning that they had merely streamed through and out the other side. Dennis's misery was not for me to hasten; and certainly, by the hangdog way in which he slumped back upstairs to the House of Blues, I could tell the mall was taking its toll. He seemed to be aging. Even his ponytail had begun to droop.

Meanwhile I was formulating a plan. With an accomplice to distract K. Sohail I could infiltrate her office and get a look at those tapes, and perhaps even erase any footage that might implicate me in the crime. Back at my quarters that afternoon I put the final touches on a perfunctory Progress Report, one whose insincerity felt palpable but which, at least for now, would suffice to fill the requirements of my residency before Dennis and I set our insurrection in motion. Only a matter of time, I thought, as the lights went down. The chicken teens trotted past, followed by Dennis with a lacklustre wave—and at last K. Sohail, hauling the gate across my quarters and bolting it fast.

I waited, breath held—despite myself, despite everything.

And then: *Goodnight.*

I clung to the word as she vanished, clutching it to my heart as a shipwrecked victim might some salvaged flotsam or jetsam, with the ocean heaving infinitely all around . . .

That night I had a terrible dream.

In it I woke up in my quarters to hissing from somewhere out in the mall. Pale blue shreds of light filtered in from the hallway as if illuminating a path toward me. I sat up. Listened intently: the hissing grew louder, brisker. I lay there, unmoving, hoping stillness would render me undetectable from whatever menace approached.

Yet closer still it came.

Now just outside my quarters. Now seeming to spill through the slats of the gate. Now approaching the screen, the sound turned hungry, somehow bristly . . .

I thought with horror that K. Sohail's imprisonments might not be to keep me in, but to keep something out. And whatever it was had arrived, ruffling around the screen into my sleeping area.

At first I saw nothing, only sensed a change in the atmosphere—a sort of tightening as the presence closed in. But then in the faint blue light I noticed the floor darkening—what I first took to be a shadow heralding the advance of some huge and hungry creature. But then, as it crept toward me, I realized that the darkness was what had made the sound. An oil slick, I thought. But no. It seethed in a way no liquid could. Ants?

No. Worse. Hair.

A great dark drift hungrily gobbled the tiles, rippling toward me in bed with a malevolent whisper. Not the pelt of some creature but a thing itself, *a thing made of hair*, a seething, living carpet of the stuff, with a sentience that urged it forward—or perhaps simply with an urge to find me. And I couldn't move. In the dream I was frozen, unable to flee, to roll away to safety—to scream.

It was all so fast: the hair-thing reached the foot of my bed and up it climbed, claiming the bedframe, capturing my feet and slithering up my legs, over my chest, down my arms, the coarse texture seeming to hook into my skin, each hair finding a pore, pushing inward so that it spread through me, inside me, choking organs and bones as well as skin. It reached my neck, came curling up over my chin and clamped over my mouth like a woolly mittened hand, threading into my nostrils, congesting my sinuses . . .

Everywhere, everything was consumed with wiry, surging hair.

And all the while that sound: hissing, whispering, rustling. Ravenous.

Finally the thing pried open my lips and began pouring down my throat, streaming inside me, filling my body as hair filled the room, a great tide that spread up the walls and across the ceiling, until at last the terrible finale: the hair closed over my eyes, pinning them shut, and I ceased to see anything at all—just blackness, that scrabbling blackness, as if the hair was its own kind of night.

PROGRESS REPORT #2

Is there any greater joy in life than a haircut?

One day you wake and sense that things are a little shaggy up top and around the ears, and possibly also at the rear end of your head, and that your neck has accumulated an unsightly sprouting of fur—but not to despair, for there exist seasoned professionals who know how to help with such matters. Also beards. Ladies or gents, no matter.

You head for the salon confident that you'll return a "satisfied customer," for cutting, by its very nature, assures a reduction in length. Little else in life offers such an inbuilt guarantee. Even a lunch, should it flee your system via propulsive evacuation, might leave you hungrier than you were before you ate.

Immediately upon entering the salon you are greeted by a great cheer from staff and customers alike. They know about you. And the conversations in these places are always lively and ricochet about like a bullet misfired in a rubber room. Local sports teams, the weather and hair are common topics of discussion, with everyone's opinions carried aloft on the vibrant rhythm of snipping scissors. It's like a dance. A dance of cutting and words.

An opening interaction might go something like this: "Do you want your hair cut by Jenny?" No, you prefer Lenny. "Sorry, Lenny's busy." Well, fine, you'll wait, eyeing Jenny suspiciously is that bloodlust in her eyes in the mirror? Best to never know. Besides, Lenny exudes an artful confidence with his scissors, even twirling them about in exuberant flourishes between snips. And what a moustache. He's a real pro, in other words, and you trust him not to slice off your ear and scream profanities into the gaping hole.

At this point, a good strategy is to simply settle into one of the comfortable seats in the "waiting sector," which is often helpfully equipped with a hat/coat rack for your hat, coat or other hangable accoutrements. Best, however, to hold on to your wallet, as few people, especially those swooning in the ecstasy of post-haircut bliss, can ever be trusted.

Best of all are the magazines. These have exciting names like *Yes!* and *What the Stars Did* and *Yet Another Week of Sport*. Apart from tantalizing rumours, these perpetuate useful tidbits applicable to the marginally curious and furiously desperate alike. How white might you bleach your teeth—as white as *this* thing? What flavours are this year's "foods"? Who's disgraced the nation now? And the pictures! Page after riveting page of nothing but cheekbones and divinely sculpted eyebrows, not to mention fascinating products the likes of which you'd never thought possible. Sunscreen for babies! Diapers for men!

Oh, look, the chair is open. Lenny—though obviously everyone has their own "Lenny," whatever you might call him, whether it's "Emma" or "Bruce the Impaler" or "Señor Cuts"—is beckoning you with a curling finger. The last customer's hair-debris has been swept away and disposed of somewhere—gathered in a gigantic garbage bag probably. Anyway, into the chair you go. Lenny flings a cape over you like a tarp over a corpse and buckles it snugly at your throat. It's all about to begin.

How shall it be? Short on the sides? Long in the back? Spiky up top? Or velvety and useful like the soft down of a baby seal? Lenny can do it all. "The usual," you say with confidence, as Lenny knows you so painfully well. And here come the scissors: menacing, maybe, if you didn't trust him so implicitly with your life. In less civilized hands those glinting blades would be instruments of death. Not so with Lenny. Not here. Not now. Likely never.

God, look at all that hair drifting down around you. It's a type of ballet. A spritz from Lenny's "bottle of stuff" moistens the scalp for even more refined trimming. He asks non-imposing questions, which you answer normally per your mastery of social decorum. Or else he silently plies his trade on your head. At a nudge you tilt obediently to accommodate Lenny's favourite angles. In the mirror you watch yourself transformed from a stupid, hairy clown who stumbled in off the street into an elegant swan—or better.

And now for the moment of truth. The scissors calm and settle. Lenny produces a mirror to show you the back. It's perfect. Everything about it is absolutely perfect. That moustachioed genius has done it again. You wipe away a grateful tear. "Yes," you whisper, which is all you can manage.

As Lenny brushes some stray clippings from your face and retrieves his cape, applause resounds around the shop. But he's unfazed. It's simply what a craftsman of his calibre does.

All in a day of, as they say, making work.

TOWARD THE END OF MY THIRD WEEK, Dennis failed to show up for lunch. Our noon-hour meals had become regular and, I'd thought, requisite daily check-ins at which we broke bread—or, rather, chicken—and discussed our respective disappointments in the mall (all while I observed him for further signs of existential collapse). So as I sat at "our" table with an entire bird cooling before me, grease congealing in a lardy paste amid the leaves, I was confused and even a bit hurt by his absence.

Had I done something wrong? Driven Dennis away with an untoward comment? Repulsed him somehow (physically, morally . . . sensually)? Perhaps he had sensed my longing for K. Sohail's nightly send-off, turned jealous and was now smearing my name around the mall. Or what if he were exclusively a "leg man" and had suffered silently every time I split our chicken? This thought illuminated a broader truth: I'd failed to notice a comrade in trouble. I pictured Dennis, forsaken and ignored, left with no recourse but to hang himself by a fashionable belt from the rafters of the House of Blues.

In which case, I'd killed him. Hardly the work of a best friend!

Sentence by sentence I replayed our last conversation for an ill-considered word or phrase that Dennis might have construed as offensive or alienating. It could have been anything. As I've made clear, my interpersonal fluency is a "work in progress," and I worry that my limitations manifest sociopathically. So some inadvertently botched basic exchange (e.g., Dennis: *Good morning*. Me: *Die a slow death*.) could well have provoked a vengeful campaign against yours truly—or worse.

Yet perhaps it was nothing I said, or even did, but instead a revelation about me that had driven him away. Some gesture or tic could have cracked the carapace that concealed my true self, one unknown even to me, and afforded Dennis a glimpse into my soul. And maybe what he saw there looked deviant—or devious.

Well, there was this: during our last meeting, Dennis had noticed my ring. Since I'd donned it for good the week prior, the ring had become such a habitual part of my get-up that I'd more or less forgotten its existence, so when Dennis asked about it, my first instinct was to conceal it beneath the table as if apprehended amid some terrible deceit. Realizing how suspicious this seemed, I coolly returned my hand to the tabletop. Oh, I said, turning it this way and that, *this* old thing?

It's pretty, said Dennis; I told him thanks. But the way he was peering at the ring struck me as more than sartorial curiosity. He seemed . . . covetous. But also as if he were trying to see *beyond* the ring to discover its—and my—secrets. So I remarked that the chicken was getting cold, brandished my cutlery like a warrior and set to it with focused, and I hoped contagious, fury.

But Dennis wouldn't let the subject drop. How had I acquired a ring so lavish, he wanted to know, and under what circumstances, and was it expensive, and had I paid for it on something he, ever the professional, called "layaway," and if so were the payments weekly or monthly, and so on. I shrugged and deflected his inquiries with beleaguered laughter, a sound meant to suggest humility—sure, the ring was indeed exquisite, Dennis, but was it really appropriate to dwell on such luxuries here in the mall's skylit food court over this humble meal of teen-roasted chicken?

Yet all the while the phrase *rightful owner* looped through my thoughts. The ring wasn't mine, really. Nor was I its. And from his unrelenting inquisition, it seemed that Dennis sensed my unworthiness and was attempting to tease out the truth. But why should a chance discovery be party to some moral compact? Shouldn't an owner's carelessness cede their rights to property? A statement like *you are mine*, per the standard caprices of human love, could be directed at anyone in its path: here it goes for a while, and fades, and one retreats to the basement with a blanket, emerging finally like some amorous mole seeking a new and better target. You are mine, and now *you* are mine, and now *you*—on it goes. Why not the same for rings?

Dennis had turned even more intent. He leaned across the table and, with a look that suggested re-evaluation of my ethical stature in the mall, eyed me steadily. He seemed to require an answer. So I gave him one.

It's an engagement ring, I said simply. I'm engaged to be married.

Dennis pushed back from the table as if the words were a bomb and he'd been repelled by the shockwave. But then he turned curious again: Who was the lucky gal or fella? He was after a name. In a panic I provided one, beginning with a syllable that floated to the surface of my mind and then scrambling from it to another, and another, until I'd reached the end of some plausible human nomenclature: Klass-an-der-ell-a.

Klassanderella? That was my fiancée's name? Dennis had never heard it before; where was she from?

The islands, I told him cryptically, gesturing southeast.

Dennis made a noise like *ah* and returned to his chicken with a faint smile.

And that had, more or less, been the end of the conversation.

Now, with Dennis "missing in action," I wiped my grease-splattered fingers on a napkin and considered that smile. In the moment I'd thought he'd seemed impressed—cowed, even—and, should he pursue the story, I quickly readied an entire life for this alleged Klassanderella, back in the islands with her family: her mother was sick, which was why despite our betrothal Klassanderella was there, and I here. Every day she tended the poor bedridden woman, fanning her with a massive palm leaf and dribbling coconut milk between her parched lips, and Klassanderella's father was a fisherman who in the evenings would haul his skiff up onto the beach and trundle ashore with a pole yoked over his shoulders draped with fat, glistening sea bass, and Klassanderella would get a fire going where she'd roast one of those bass in another palm leaf, with coconut, while the rest went on ice for the following day at market, to which Klassanderella would hike through a jungle teeming with leopards and the fish in a basket balanced expertly on her head, and for the rest of the day she'd slave away at her fishmonger's stall, hawking her wares in a hoarsening voice—wait, was "hoarsening" a word? As in to become hoarse? I worried that it might imply that Klassanderella suffered an equine aspect, which couldn't be further from the truth! No, she was beautiful and humane, and fiercely intelligent, and an excellent salesperson too, and careful, and every night before bed she took a moment to admire the majestic, perfectly crafted ring on her finger, an exact replica of the one her husband-to-be wore on his own hand in a mall so many thousand miles away to the distant northwest, and she was his and he was hers, and the rings were theirs together.

The ring really was splendid. It shone in the lights of the food court like a beacon (to a faraway lover) and looked as natural on my hand as the nails at the ends of each finger. And in partnership with my new jeans the ring vaulted my "look" into the heights of haute couture. But was it absurd to be dressing like some sort of baron or playboy in the plebeian confines of the mall? Klassanderella aside, might the ring *and* the jeans seem, to Dennis, for example, like an excessive costume designed to elevate me above my surroundings and/or disguise my actually deficient soul?

Perhaps *that* was what Dennis sensed—my disingenuousness, my ostentation—and, as a good and honest fellow struggling to make a go of it in the high-stakes world of commerce, denim division, he felt that my pretensions were compromising him. He could even, quite reasonably, extrapolate that the downfall of the House of Blues might be due to an association with me, its first and heretofore only customer, a poseur who had sullied the store's reputation by not only dominating "opening day" but making off with the finest jeans in Dennis's entire stock.

Suddenly the chicken had a charred and bitter taste. I could eat no more. I ditched more than half my lunch (plus Dennis's untouched portion, even his precious leg) into the garbage and returned to my quarters, hoping that "making work" might bolster my spirits. My third Progress Report was due soon. But what would it survey? Surely not this.

THE FOLLOWING DAY, when again Dennis failed to meet me for lunch, I forwent the gloom of another solo meal and headed up to the second floor, emboldened now by resentment.

Who did this Dennis think he was, when I'd been so hospitable and "shown him the ropes" at the mall, frequented his business, extended the hand of friendship, shared a coop's-worth of chickens, and let him in on my imminent marriage to Klassanderella? I would march up to his House of Blues and give that ungrateful hotshot a piece of my mind. Though once I reached the top of the escalator my gait dwindled from retributive stride to shameful slink, and in a sort of gnarled scuttle I made my way past Kookaburra (shuttered) and sundry other ruined businesses until I arrived at the House of Blues, into which I peeked sneakily, concealed behind a pillar.

The lights were off. The gates were closed. And inside the store: nothing. No Dennis, no jeans. The place had been cleared out. The shelves were barren. The cash register hung open like the gaping jaw of a recently guillotined head. Had Dennis enjoyed some sort of sales bonanza and "sold out"?

Despite everything—the desertion, the pain—my heart leapt. Dennis! His absence might have nothing to do with me at all. Perhaps he was simply off on a business trip replenishing his stock, visiting the finest denim wholesalers across the land, or heading right to the source at the factory, fingering still-warm jean jackets as they came tumbling off the line, or even to the fields to kneel in the dirt and sniff the budding cotton, selecting only the finest crops per his refined and exacting taste.

But my heart's leap was feeble and vain; the next beat plunged to my guts. What sales bonanza? To whom? Some spectral public that I'd somehow missed, let alone failed to engage? Absurd. The mall was no place for glory. It was a great, windowless garburator that made a mulch of dreams. Had it crushed Dennis's too? Was he at home, now, fetally curled on the floor, sobbing at his folly and cursing me for failing to warn him? But was I really the one to blame, Dennis? A modest temporary resident of the mall, assigned a pitiable existence engaging a public that barely existed, documenting those few and same instances in wildly dishonest reports? Still, gazing into the evacuated shop, I felt a pang of melancholy. Poor, tragic Dennis, I thought. The boy had believed!

Then I sensed movement. In the back of the store. An animal, I thought—something furry and dark scurrying around in the shadows. Maybe a rat. I moved closer, threaded my fingers through the grating, pressed my face close and peered inside.

There it was, curled around the base of Dennis's ladder. A glossy black thing, now nosing out into the light. And creeping across the floor.

I squinted. It was longer than a rat, and sleeker, more tapered. (Were minks native to shopping malls?) And then it was gone again, swallowed by shadow or perhaps crawling underneath one of the shelves. Faintly I could hear it: a scuffling, whisking sort of noise. Not the patter and ticking of a rodent's clawed feet. No, this was more fluid, as if the creature were slithering along on its belly.

It appeared again by the counter, darting a bit more actively from one patch of shadow to the next. And then it paused, seeming to gather itself—and in a sudden rush it unfurled and came hurtling across the floor, straight toward me. I sprung back as it slipped under the gate, glided over my shoe and went scrabbling off into the mall.

Was it? It couldn't be.

It was. I'd recognize that magnificent ponytail anywhere.

FOR THE BETTER PART OF THE AFTERNOON I prowled the mall for that orphaned and now sentient, or at least animated, piece of Dennis. No sign of the ponytail upstairs or down, or in the food court, or even in the toilets—a place I had previously avoided. At first I performed only a cursory inspection (cracking the door and hollering Dennis's name) before acknowledging my own cowardice; for my missing friend's sake the place required a more thorough survey.

Public restrooms are not places where I've ever felt comfortable, what with the invariable puddles of excrement and the salacious, threatening propositions scrawled all over the walls. So I entered with reticence. What struck me first was the light—blinding, consuming, and as shocking as stepping into a icy bath. The door closed behind me, sealing me in. Everything was white: the tiled floor and walls, the stalls, the sinks, even the *smell*, somehow, and the fluorescents overhead buzzed so intensely that they seemed to produce the very sound of light.

My senses acclimatized. The initial shock passed. Now that I could see it, the bathroom was really quite impressive. It was so clean. After the dimly lit claustrophobia of the mall, this felt . . . emptying. And though my feet were soundly on the ground, all that whiteness, like some miasmic fog, made me feel I was amid the clouds and floating.

The bathroom seemed somehow detached from the mall—and perhaps the universe. An antechamber. A vestibule of the soul with its atmosphere of purity and sanitation, its soothing antiseptic odour of chlorine. And in it I too detached from the world—and then myself. I lost all sense of time and space. I forgot my purpose. I was airy and unburdened, adrift. I might have been grinning. I gazed into all that light and had no thoughts, none at all, and the trance was broken only when the toilets came alive with a roar and their contents were vacuumed into the bowels of the mall.

Out I reeled into the food court's drab luminescence, my vision spangled and pyrotechnic. I had to steady myself on the counter of the chicken restaurant, the teens looking on. Something had swept me away in there, behind the door marked with graphics of a man and woman standing side by side. Those silhouettes struck me now as illustrations of myself: an outline, gutted of being, reduced to nothing but form. Who knew a simple bathroom visit could inspire such reveries!

And I'd also confirmed that Dennis's ponytail wasn't loose in there. Not only, amid all that whiteness, would it have stood out like a stain, but a shag of dead cells had no business tarnishing such purity. No offence to its former owner.

What a fool I'd been to have never scouted the toilets before,

I thought, returning to my quarters. Nearly three weeks into my residency and only now was I discovering their clarifying properties. Who knew what other secrets lay out there in the mall? Back at my workstation I set to writing a Progress Report with vigour—something impressionistic to codify the day's experience. Something for myself.

But before I could write a word, my gaze snagged on the ring on my hand. Klassanderella! My heart fluttered, overcome with longing. I pictured my beloved down there in the islands, tending to her ailing mother, not to mention all that fishmongering on the side. What commitment. What a woman! I was lucky to have her, even at such a distance. And our wedding would be splendid, a truly wonderful affair—wine and dancing and a goat, traditionally slaughtered in a bloodbath in the sand.

Such longing I felt then, such anticipation. Love: the rope of the hangman, dangling loosely around our necks! But before that thrilling lurch to the gallows, I would have to soldier through to the end of the residency. In just over six weeks it would be over and my beloved and I could at last reunite, falling into each other's arms with gratitude and breathless, succulent kisses. I could fairly smell Klassanderella's hair (a marine bouquet, also coconut) as I imagined our reunion, and smiled wistfully. What a good and graceful thing it was, I thought, not to be alone.

AND WHERE WAS K. SOHAIL amid all this? The only times I saw her were those brief appearances at my quarters to unleash me in the morning and, in the evening, to offer a tender, dare I say affectionate goodnight. How the woman spent her days was a mystery. Did she simply sit at the monitors? Or stalk the halls undetected like a beige-suited spectre? Or might she not caretake the mall at all, and in fact relocate her talents elsewhere?

The last night of the week, waiting for K. Sohail to collect my Progress Report (an idle and vain thing, I felt, that failed to really capture the essence of the Episode of Existential Sanctification in the Toilets), I sat at my desk thinking about her, and Dennis, and Dennis's runaway ponytail—what a day!—and as my thoughts drifted around the mall they settled on the service elevator: specifically on its undesignated third button. The mall had another floor! A basement or sub-level. What was down there? Or who?

Here she came—the flashlight, the jingle, the squeak. My Progress Report wordlessly accepted, the gate pulled across my quarters and locked fast. The tantalizing silence. And here my usual anticipation was overcome with sudden guilt. Was I "two-timing" Klassanderella? Surely the tenderness between me and the caretaker wouldn't sit well if exposed at the altar—if, say, K. Sohail stormed our beachfront wedding with a satchel full of video evidence and chastened poor Klassanderella with the truth.

So instead of waiting for K. Sohail to fill the space with her nightly benediction, I pre-empted her.

How was your day, I asked, conventionally enough.

The query seemed to strike K. Sohail like a blow to the gut; her body even buckled a bit. She sighed, closed her eyes. Pressed her forehead to the grating. Stayed like that for a while. What had I done? I waited in terror, expecting some sort of reprimand. But when she at last opened her eyes, she only shuddered, as if whatever she felt were a cloak from which she might shake herself free.

Long, she said.

I'd never heard a word sound so tired.

But before I could probe any further, K. Sohail glanced at the security camera and in a broken voice offered a rushed, garbled goodnight and—there's no other word—fled.

What conflict I felt, retreating behind the screen. Of course, for the sake of my marriage to Klassanderella it was preferable not to be whispered at lovingly every bedtime, but even so I felt . . . betrayed. K. Sohail's goodnight had been dispatched like trash down a garbage chute. And then she'd run! As if making an escape!

First Dennis, and now my only other companion in the mall. What was I doing to people? Had my simple question prompted an emotional meltdown? Were all of K. Sohail's days so long? Perhaps she was in love with me, and my casual pre-emption of her goodnight had revealed that my heart was in fact sworn to another (i.e., Klassanderella), and the shame of adultery had sent her packing.

But no, that wasn't it, I thought, replaying the moments before she absconded. What bothered her most was that our exchange was being caught on tape.

The pieces fell into place. K. Sohail was a consummate professional. She performed her duties in the mall with forbearance and dignity. My thoughtless question had punctured that veneer and everything had collapsed. Her flight suggested dishonour . . . but also something more troubling. She'd bolted, I was certain, to escape the mall's all-seeing eye. Who was watching? Who was in control? What were the consequences for K. Sohail being emotionally compromised? Termination? (Of her career—surely not of her life?)

And then a realization struck.

I'd not heard the telltale click that heralded my nightly imprisonment. Amid all the drama, K. Sohail had forgotten to lock me in.

I slipped out of bed to the gate.

Indeed: unsecured, and flapping as loosely as a broken wing.

Freedom beckoned.

What was out there? All the threads of my mall-bound existence seemed to float amid the blue-tinged gloom. Dennis, K. Sohail, the *Now you are mine* ring, the hair in my tongue, even the endless chicken . . . Collectively, they braided into the arterial system of some diabolical creature. Somewhere in the mall pulsed its heart. And here I was now, alone—observed no doubt by some ghostly power, but with a chance to finally do something. To seek the truth. To truly engage. To work. To progress. To do, to know, to make, to be!

The mall at night, bathed in the blue phosphorescence of an aquarium and as still as a crypt, felt even more bewildering than it did during the day. After opening the gate just enough to slip out, like a weirdo in a trance I stalked the empty hallway, with the security cameras and whoever sat at the other end of them watching me go.

The air seemed to pulse with a kind of aura, something thick and almost viscous that churned around me as I passed the dead fountain, searching the shadows for the corridor that led to the service elevator. But the lighting was so dim that I reached the food court without finding the entrance. Figuring that I must have missed it, I turned around and headed back the direction I'd come, eyes "peeled."

However. Proceeding straight ahead, ostensibly away from the food court in the direction of my quarters, passing shops that now, in the pale aquatic light, seemed even more identically shuttered and abandoned, and failing again to find the corridor, I somehow ended up back at the food court. Via the skylight a lunar pallor washed over everything, and I stood amid it feeling more disoriented than ever. Had I turned around without realizing? Or, like a fool lost in the desert, begun listing to one side and walked an inadvertent circuit?

I turned around again, eyes trained straight ahead. The security lights faded to a vanishing point maybe twenty yards away. Then there was just blackness. But I'd walked that passage dozens of times and knew my way from one end to the other. A straight

line. No real trick to it. So off I went. Yet what emerged at the
end of that tunnel into the shadows was again the blasted food
court! Somehow I was looping around in circles. Never mind the
security corridor, at this rate how would I get back to bed? What
if K. Sohail were to discover me here in the morning, clad in
obvious nightclothes? Might my scantily clad escape, on camera,
condemn us both?

The only solution seemed to be heading upstairs to try a
different path. The escalator was shut down for the night, so by
my own power I ascended to the second floor. Here the lighting
was even weaker, without continuity: one trembling blue lamp,
a gap of darkness, and then the next. A left turn from the top of
the escalator led me through these intermittent puddles of light
past Kookaburra, the sunflowers looming monstrously in the
vitrine, and on. I paused for a moment at the House of Blues
and gazed inside: gloom and stillness and a taut sort of silence,
with a stain of feeble light struggling to reach inside. It felt like
a view from the water's edge down through the depths to some
netherworld beyond.

On I went.

K. Sohail's office was, ostensibly at least, amid the next block
of stores. But these were lost in darkness; if there were security
lights in this stretch of hallway, they were out. So I put my hand
to the wall to guide myself and stepped into the nothing of it. The
brick was cool against my fingertips as I stepped, one socked foot
and then the next, and groped for some break or turn that might
indicate the security corridor.

I paused and looked back: the lights sputtered, flashed and
snuffed out. The entire upper floor was cast in total pitch. I couldn't

see anything: not the stores around me, not the escalator, not a hand before my face. So I reached out again to touch the wall, to steady myself—but what I touched wasn't brick.

It was . . . springy. It was hair.

I lurched away from the wall and into the darkness, my hand still prickling. I could hear something now, a bristly sort of noise.

The hair, I sensed, was crawling.

I began staggering back the way I'd come—and must have made some sort of turn, because my extended hands encountered the wall again—or what was no longer wall but a seething pelt. Even as I recoiled I could feel the curls grasping to snag my flesh. On I stumbled, seeing nothing, all that hair rustling over the walls and chasing me along.

After a few lurching steps my shoulder struck the wall again, and a few dozen hairs clung to my shirt. I had to tear myself away, careering off in some new direction. I began to run through the dark, hands out. It felt like falling, like some terrible tumble down a chasm into the earth, chased by that scuffling hiss, a thousand infernal secrets whispered in the dark. Closer it came, and closer—and then I smacked face-first into something hard and cold.

The elevator door!

My hand found the call button. Slammed it as hard as I could. Amid the hiss of the hair came a grinding sound, a clang. I grasped for the leather thong and tugged open the doors. Dove inside and pulled them closed. Darkness in here too; all the lights were out. The hissing on the other side reached the doors and turned furious. Soon it would find the cracks and begin spilling in. I swept my hands over the steel panel beside the door and thumbed the first button I found. A glowing coin of light appeared in the dark: the unnamed floor.

And with a growl and a cranking of chains I was off.

Down to the first floor—and past it.

Down and down I dropped, toward the basement, wherever it was, and whatever or whoever awaited me there.

PROGRESS REPORT #3

Ah! Is there anything so clean and rejuvenating as milk? As pure and white as fresh-fallen snow before a heedless farmer tramps across it in dung splattered boots. From the moment each delectable drop is yanked free from the unsuspecting cow to the glorious occasion when the first splash kisses your lips, there's nothing quite like it. Cold, smooth and perfectly wet: milk. Verb and noun: milk the milk! Sir or madam, whomsoever you please, milk it until the cows come home and cannibalistically demand a sip of their own delicious juices. It's definitely something to think about, milk.

Or, say, clouds. And not the derelict, rain-stained ones that glub morosely across the sky or else hang, heavy and guileless, like a half-assed taunt from a cowardly god. No, I'm talking about the fluffy white type. Clouds, that is. Darling steamy puffs. Each one as joy-filled as a child's laugh—and not the evil kind brayed across the classroom at a moronic peer. No, the clouds I'm talking about are like a noiseless song that no one can hear—not even you. Light as air and illusively solid: tempting as it may seem, walk upon clouds at your peril. Something else to consider is clouds.

Also snow, actual snow. Whether floating down blissfully from the heavens or spilled all over the ground like a thick, frosty layer of petrified milk. But why cry over fallen snow? No, you should laugh. Or preferably be quiet. You should just stare out your window in reverential silence and admire all that virginal beauty, like a pair of jeans fresh from the shop: creased in all the right places, untarnished by grubby human skin. So clean and great. Snow.

What I'm getting at here is that bathroom decor isn't some slapdash endeavour. Attention to detail makes all the difference.

A bathroom should be a sanctuary. An escape of sorts. A chance to make oneself anew. The effect you're going for is serenity, per the milk/cloud/snow "metaphors" above.

White isn't a colour, technically, but rather an absence of colour (or else all the colours prismed together—unclear), so that's the colour to keep in mind. Also the whole idea of absence: you want the bathroom to be about what's *not* in it. For example, how your overweight, pork-chop-crazed uncle had his way in there for a good forty-five minutes, his struggles and triumphs expressed so grotesquely that you had to turn up the radio in the other room. That should never be on anyone's mind again, and no evidence of his visit should remain.

You want a bathroom to convey purity, no matter how foul the visits of previous barbarians. Details aside, what actually happens in a bathroom? We are cleansed. Inside and out. The bowels or bladder are discreetly voided, but also the teeth are scrubbed clean and so is the body. Some people prettify themselves in the mirror with combs, "product," tiny scissors and rouge. To each their own!

Think of the various terms deployed for that special place: restroom, as in a place of rest; bathroom, as in a place with a bath in it; washroom, connoting somewhere to wash yourself of filths both literal and figurative. All are true. No one would dare tarnish that hallowed space by calling it a "pooping house" or "shame chamber," except maybe a child who specializes in insolence. And they should be corrected—gently, of course, for they know no better.

But we—the initiated, the wise, the consecrated—know better, don't we? About bathrooms, and what they can and should be, and how the experience can transform our lives? Yes. Yes, we certainly do.

THE ELEVATOR TRIP TOOK, I think, hours. Eventually I sat on the floor. Wherever I was being taken was not simply a basement level below the mall. No, the destination was burrowed far beneath the surface of the earth. At times the path twisted—not plummeting straight down but angling one way and then rounding a corner, even travelling horizontally for great distances, only to descend again.

At a steady chug the elevator travelled to wherever the mysterious button commanded, its golden glow the only light in the car. At some point I must have dozed off, because I was jolted awake by a great thump and a chattering of metal, and I found myself sprawled face down, drool streaking my cheek.

Up I got and hesitantly opened the doors. In streamed light so ferociously glaring it was as if the sun itself perched at the threshold. I leapt back, retinas scalded. Even closed eyes were no match for this conflagration: the back of each eyelid blazed, each capillary articulated in wormy squiggles against a backdrop the colour of raw meat. Bravely I cracked my eyes and through the slits permitted the light in shreds. Gradually that searing whiteness began to settle into a visual field.

What I saw: the elevator opened to a corridor tiled in white, lit blazingly in a style identical to the food court bathroom. Same tiles, same sterility. But here there were no fixtures, just a tunnel of gleaming ceramic squares that narrowed to a vanishing point some indeterminable distance away.

What else to do? I followed it.

As I had in the bathroom, I felt disembodied, as if I were floating along inside a cloud. Nothing tarnished the corridor's monochrome. Not even security cameras.

For the first time in weeks, I was not being watched.

At last free from observation, I might, if so inclined, perform any private humiliation I wished. Some sort of nude dance or prance or a series of occult gesticulations, or I might utter a confession so compromising that under normal circumstances it would prompt a fatal leap from a bridge or cliff.

Or I could just scream and scream.

So I screamed.

But no sooner had the word left my lips than those beautiful syllables—*Klassanderella!* —came caroming so forcefully back down the corridor that a breeze ruffled my exquisite haircut, and the echo produced an echo, which produced another, each reverberation doubling upon itself and folding in and booming out until it all bled together and a roar of white noise engulfed the corridor, the name of my beloved garbled into something so alien and overwhelming that it drove me to my knees, my hands over my ears, and even then the sound continued to refract and replicate through a low drone into a sound I can only describe as the

howling of some ghoul or demon, a howling that consumed me—
that consumed my *soul*—crouched in the corridor with my head
between my knees, assaulted by a monster into which my own
voice had breathed life and which was dragging me down into its
infernal lair, a hell of unimaginable horror, of implacable madness
and suffering such as no living soul has ever known, and even as
this creature opted for mercy and the reverberations began to
fade—to a growl, to a murmur, and finally to a hiss—I sensed that
an essential part of me had been taken there.

Amid this new silence I unclenched my body and stood.
Looked up and down the hall. Nothing remained of that terrible
sound: no tremor in the air, no flickering of the lights; the corridor
was as still and open as an unblinking eye. From the open elevator
to the distant end of the passageway, or what I could make out as
the end, far off in the distance, there was nothing but what struck
me as a kind of gloating sanctimony: the corridor had shown me
its power, lest I try to disturb it.

So with new-found reverence I continued in my pyjamas. Not
that my admiration for the corridor's serenity was without prece-
dent. All the way back to the episode in the food court bathroom, as
I hope I've conveyed, I'd appreciated the pristine decor and ambi-
ence. Though perhaps I hadn't fully appreciated my fortune, as a
flawed and morally derelict human, to be permitted into such pristine conditions, sullying its cleansing atmosphere with my every
revolting breath. Never mind staining the white corridor with my
ugly human voice! What a fool I'd been to try to assert my putrid
existence, even by shouting out the name of the woman I loved.

It didn't matter where the corridor was taking me, or if it led
nowhere at all. Simply existing in it was a gift. If the purgatory of

the mall had been a test, its trials had brought me here, to a state of pure being. The food court bathroom had been a glimpse into this glorious annihilation of selfhood. And here I could journey fully through or into an infinitude in which I might become, at last, nothing: not a person, not a jeans enthusiast, not a fiancé, not a resident, not a subject or object or anything. Now I might at last walk—or, more so, drift—into obliteration, into irrelevance, until I was little more than a vagueness of form, an outline of a person, without aim or destination. And perhaps eventually, not even that, in this corridor to nowhere, to oblivion and beyond . . .

Oh, actually it led to a swimming pool.

The corridor dead-ended at an eye-level window about six inches around, and the view through it was underwater. Glowing bulbs in the swimming pool's walls cast quavering beams that rippled up to the surface maybe fifteen feet above. Though the tiles were also white, the pool had a bluish tinge that felt, even on the far side of the glass, satisfying in the way of anything that fulfills its destiny: the quintessence of a peach being peachy, a strongman twirling an extravagant moustache, a dog defecating on a manicured lawn with a glimmer of triumph in its otherwise soulless eyes.

I am not a swimmer. Never have been. Oh, certainly there was a time in my youth when I was the requisite "man overboard" on any boat trip from one port to another, and I held my own amid the sharks until a buoyant ring was flung from the decks and I was dragged for miles—punitively, I assume. But I'd never dive in willingly, and I have always admired those with an inclination or knack for steering their bodies deliberately through the waves:

there, these people aspire from the shoreline and, through some miraculous thrashing of limbs, attain the horizon, and beyond.

So it was with great longing that I gazed through the porthole (portal?) into the swimming pool. The longing of dreams unfulfilled, or even dreams undreamt. And of course Klassanderella. Having grown up in the islands, she was an expert swimmer: from great clifftop heights she'd blithely plunge into the depths and frolic through fields of coral and great billowing throngs of sea life with her breath bubbling in wild percolations, and then she'd surface to croon a mournful siren song that coaxed kind sailors around an unexpected sandbar or promontory, or else seduced dastards to their rocky deaths.

We were different, sure, but isn't it precisely those gaps in which love, like a weed between paving stones, blooms and thrives? Yes, it was Klassanderella's nautical proficiency that made us such perfect partners. Imagine if I were drowning. She could save me. And would! Gazing through that porthole or portal into the swimming pool, I humoured the tantalizing thought that, were I to picture my beloved persistently and precisely enough, I might conjure her—fluttering up to the portal or porthole, our hands touching but for a pane of glass between them, until at last the longing in her eyes turned wild with panic and she was forced to surface for air. For even love has its limits. Among them, suffocation and death.

But of course no one appeared. My mind was too weak to summon much of anything. The pool remained empty, the surface shivering slightly as if it were a living thing, its movements as tremulous as human breath—as the breath of a loved one (i.e., Klassanderella) on your cheek as they sleep.

I looked around for a door or hatch that might allow me to pass into the room with the swimming pool—god forbid into the swimming pool itself! I ran my hands all over the wall, feeling for a catch. Nothing! No handle or knob in sight. No catch, no hatch, no latch, no keyhole or keypad, and nothing to suggest a secret passage tripped with a canny nudge or caress. Just tiles from floor to ceiling.

Surely this couldn't be it—a dead end. I looked back at the elevator down the other end of the corridor with its doors hanging open. Why did it bring me here? As spectacles go, the portal/porthole's view of the swimming pool was briefly enchanting but ultimately limited. There wasn't even anyone swimming! Or boat traffic, or fish.

But then I felt the sprout on my tongue and remembered what had chased me here: the waves of hair that had consumed the second floor of the mall. I shuddered. An escape from that ravenous carpet to the relative sanctity of this corridor, however boring, wasn't so bad. Back up in the mall, my hirsute predator might be lying in wait. But I couldn't hide out down here forever, especially if K. Sohail were to discover me missing. She might already have done so—it was impossible to know how long I'd slept.

Movement in the portal/porthole caught my eye.

A glimmer, a flash. A shadow, maybe, of some fleeting creature—a man, a woman, a fish, a thing. Pressing my face to the glass, I craned my neck back and forth but could make out nothing, just the shimmering blue water speared and spangled with bands of light. A stillness that moved. The natural tremor of the waves, or a wake left by something that had disturbed the water?

Then I saw it, up on the surface in silhouette: a human, floating into view. Just a shape with no defining features, such that it was impossible to tell if the person was swimming face down or on their back. I tapped the glass, hollered. No response: whoever it was only rotated slightly in the current, arms and legs splayed.

My god, might it be K. Sohail, out for a morning dip? So this is what she got up to all day! I'd taken her for such a hard worker, a dedicated servant of the mall, and here she was—as she might well be every morning—leisurely "taking the waters." Who knew how else she wasted her days? Foot massages, bouts of vigorous perspiration in a steam room, a tea service replete with cakes, maybe even a nap. I eyed her up there—floating, hanging—with feelings of betrayal. Oh, K. Sohail, you scoundrel. You rogue! While I'd never claim perspicacity as one of my finer qualities, I'd been duped—the keys, the uniform, the focus, the guise of diligence. All a ruse! A fiendish ruse!

Oh, but wait: the swimmer was in fact a man. A *naked* man, I discovered, as certain anatomical features drooped into a band of light. And not swimming so much as simply drifting face down, propelled by the jet stream vomited from nozzles around the pool.

And . . . no. My god. No, it couldn't be.

It was.

Dennis.

Floating there, lifeless.

And, very clearly, very dead.

I hammered on the portal/porthole, the walls, my own chest, and hollered for all I was worth. Of course it all amounted to nothing—not even another cascade of soul-destroying reverberations from the corridor. Perhaps whatever forces ruled this place had decreed that witnessing my best friend's fate was punishment enough. So with sinking spirits I watched Dennis—or what had once been Dennis, robbed of his ponytail and life and jeans—bob along the surface of the water while the pool lights glimmered like macabre death-lamps below.

Had he drowned? For a moment I felt a little pang of envy—how had some twenty-something ingenue denim-dealer been afforded access to the pool while I, the sole and expressly anointed resident of the mall, had not?—before realizing that Dennis would surely be the jealous one now, were he alive, since I was alive and he wasn't. This thought made my brain twirl in vertiginous ways and I had to sit on the floor to gather myself.

Certainly the body needed to be collected, and unless K. Sohail was Dennis's murderer she'd likely need to know, as caretaker of the mall, about a corpse floating around the pool. (She likely had access to a specialized net or prong for such tasks.) And, even if she had "done him in," disposing properly of Dennis's remains would still be her responsibility. It seemed odd, at any rate, that he'd just been left there, in full view of anyone who happened upon the portal/porthole—or the pool itself, however one got on deck.

I toyed my tongue-hair over a back molar; it needed a trim. But first I would return to ground level and confront K. Sohail about Dennis. If she was a killer, fine. She'd certainly had her chances to kill me, if that was her thing, and so far had made no moves. And would someone with designs of cold-blooded murder really offer such tender goodnights? Unless she was "playing the long game," fattening me up on chicken and her affections in order to feast on my delicious meat at the end of my residency . . .

But this was absurd: K. Sohail didn't have the look of a cannibal. Not in those sneakers.

I made my way back to the elevator, pulled the door closed and hit G. Improbably enough, less than thirty seconds later the thing stopped short and that little lozenge dimmed. (Had my trip down taken some unnecessarily roundabout route?) Opening the doors, I discovered myself indeed returned to the mall's first floor. The lights were on, indicating that it was daytime—but which day? How much time had passed? I ventured down the service corridor and into the mall proper: no one, of course. Just the empty hallways, which had the same look as always—complacent, vacant, anaesthetic.

And then I heard that telltale squeak and jingle down the hall, and raced after it.

Only when I caught up to K. Sohail, riding the escalator up to her office, did I realize that I was implicating myself in my own escape. But had it really been an escape? There were no stipulations in my Acceptance Letter about venturing into the mall after hours. And we'd never broached the somewhat awkward subject of K. Sohail locking me inside my quarters every night. Perhaps she did it merely out of habit, accustomed as she was to ensuring security and order. If I brought it up, she might well respond with incredulity—*I'm sorry, no, of course, please feel free to roam however you wish.*

So I called out to her with confidence from the bottom of the escalator, certain that I'd not compromised either of us.

Yet upon noticing me at the base of the escalator still in my pyjamas—a strange look passed over K. Sohail's face: the eyes went wide, the mouth slackened. Was it fear? astonishment?

wanton desire? Whatever that look intended, she fixed me with it, unblinking, as she was lifted to the second floor—as one might gaze in the mirror at, say, a hair growing from one's mouth: with paralyzed stupefaction.

And then the escalator's steps flattened out and swept the caretaker from view.

Well, I followed her, on the offensive now that K. Sohail seemed to be avoiding me. As the escalator dragged me upstairs, I sensed more and more that the "look" had been of guilt and its attendant getaway. (So she *had* killed Dennis, I thought—and perhaps now deserved a taste of her own medicine!)

By the time I reached the second floor, K. Sohail was nowhere in sight. Hiding in her office, no doubt. So I headed that way, remembering faintly my last trip here: the darkness, the bristling carpet. Now all the lights were on and the hallways were empty. And I, the once-hunted, had turned hunter—or at least a vessel of retribution and revenge.

With the pulse of justice thrumming in my chest, I pushed through the doors to the service corridor, only to discover the caretaker's office locked and empty. I peered through the window at all those monitors: dozens of shots listlessly tracked across the lifeless spaces of the mall—the food court, the fountain, my quarters, etc.—with no sign of K. Sohail in any of them. Yet one monitor in the corner of the room had a suspiciously blank screen.

She was up here somewhere. I returned to the mall proper and stood for a moment listening. There! A faint sound of voices down the hall—possibly from the House of Blues. And whom should I discover in Dennis's old shop but the murderess herself, returned to the scene of the crime. Her back to me, oblivious to my presence. So I readied my hands in a classic strangler's pose and stealthily made my approach.

And pulled up short.

She was talking to someone. My god! Was it . . . Dennis?

Perhaps he really had been only taking a dip this morning, and wasn't a drowned and bloated corpse at all. I lowered my hands. What a fool I'd been to panic, never mind nearly offing K. Sohail in misguided vengeance. So I pushed closer, eager to see over K. Sohail's shoulder—to glimpse my old comrade-in-arms, to rekindle our friendship and to apologize for forsaking him by consuming so many chickens alone.

My tongue-hair bristled. Dennis it was not.

Instead, behind a desk just like mine, perched his ponytail. Though of course now it was no longer *his*. It was simply an autonomous being: a hairstyle without a master. So no longer a ponytail at all. This was something else, something etymologically unique. Something eponymous. This was *Mr. Ponytail.*

K. Sohail stiffened a little as I loomed into her periphery, but continued talking. The words were a formless churn of sounds until I heard her mention the *requirements of the residency.* And at this my hearing sharpened, and the hair began to dance upon my tongue as if wakened, or aroused. Two meals per day would be included, K. Sohail was telling Mr. Ponytail, precisely in the terms of my Acceptance Letter.

So the dastard had killed Dennis and in lieu of punishment had been *rewarded* with a residency at the mall—presumably without even applying!—and his quarters would be his victim's old digs. The whole thing would have been perversely comical if it weren't so chilling.

I reeled out of the shop, tongue-hair wilting. A conspiracy was afoot. Had Dennis's former ponytail acted as a "lone wolf"? Or were he and K. Sohail—and possibly the honchos at the mall—somehow in cahoots? What did this mean for my own residency? I'd been "top dog" for weeks, and this new development risked relegating me to a lowly "second fiddle." What sort of work was Mr. Ponytail going to make? What were his plans for engaging the public?

I slunk back to my quarters and behind my desk.

Five weeks left of the residency. Thirty-five days, that is, before I'd be reunited with the love of my life.

The blank page gaped before me.

Death, treachery, debasement—that was the story of the mall. But was I the one to tell it? And even if I were, where would I even begin?

PROGRESS REPORT #4

‒ ‒ ‒ ‒ ‒ ‒ ‒ ‒ ‒ ‒ ‒ ‒ ‒ ‒ ‒ ‒ ‒ ‒ ‒

Where would humankind be without swimming? On land, definitely. But, more existentially, a degraded race, like the flightless chicken whose wings are good only for snacking, or a legless dog shoved around the floor. From the moment the waves kiss your naked flesh to when at last your seaweed-slathered body is washed gasping onto the sands, to swim is to live, to love and to dream. And, in many ways, to die.

Some say our ancestors were fish. Others, apes. To each his or her own, though giraffes seem out of the question. Whatever side you're on, it's undeniable that we're happiest in water. Certainly more so than amid the other elements, i.e., air (falling from a cliff), fire (incineration in a nuclear holocaust) or earth (being buried alive). A common argument suggests that drowning is a shoddy way to go, but think of it, really: embraced by the depths, tugged gently down and beckoned toward that bottomless sleep. Of all the available furniture, interesting that we call it a sea*bed*—what's more comforting than an eternal rest on that? To think you once had to be a pirate to earn a watery grave!

Unconvinced? Think of bathing—a sort of stationary, confidential swimming that happens at home. It's something we do every day. Why? Hygiene, yes, but mainly because we're not all lagoon-cavorting billionaires who take their baths under the cascading torrents of an erotic waterfall, head thrown back while shampoo, wealth and ecstasy foam all around. So we humbly fill a ceramic basin and climb on in, splashing around in our own grime until our skins pucker like sun-spoilt fruit. Then out we climb, rejuvenated, slightly cleaner, and mostly whole again.

Despite its firm appearance, the human body is made of water in some improbably high percentage—60, 70, something insane like that. Like they say: ashes to ashes, dust to dust, and moisture to the very same. Next time you see a fountain, bight, reservoir, bay, gulf, loch, tributary, canal, marsh, estuary or firth, head on in, the water's warm (actual temperature may vary). It's your calling. Just have some perspective: imagine if every wad of snot-clogged tissue were so lucky as to return to life as a tree.

Even a puddle with someone's weird sock in it! Anywhere will do, crazed as we are for even the feeblest suggestion of a swim. And whether it's a marathon haul from one shoreline to another, a daft paddle or simply dunking your arm in a toilet, those of us who crave it will pursue a dip by any means, at any cost. Our dignity, a hundred dollars—just try us. We love swimming that much.

Babies are sometimes birthed in water, a testament to the innately aquatic miracle of humankind, and also the boldness of modern medicine. What's next, nose jobs in space? But if you've ever seen a baby unleashed in a pool, eyes wide and pudgy limbs churning—such desperation! such liberty!—you've likely also had to fight the instinct, even for a moment, to dive in and haul the kid out. Curiosity beckons: Will the little gaffer make it? Usually they do.

And what of self-expression? There are as many ways to swim as there are death threats in the sea. For every shark, electric eel and whirlpool eddying down to the netherworld is a stroke for all seasons: back, front, side, some personally unique whirling this way and that. Or maybe you prefer "breast"? When it comes to swimming there are no judgments. So proceed however you desire, fiend. Friend, rather. All swimmers are friends.

In conclusion, sometimes we forget, walking around as we tend to on our legs and feet, on land, that there are other, better options. We see a river and think, "Great, where's the bridge?" Instead maybe we should just be thinking, "Great!" And then off come our clothes, discarded in a heap on the bank, and in we plunge, diving under the scum-slicked surface into that glorious rush of two hydrogens and one oxygen, times a million. And then we don't just cross to the other side (boring) but swim off somewhere down- or upstream— toward what? Who knows. Probably freedom.

MY FIFTH WEEK BEGAN with a clear intimation of what was to come.

K. Sohail released me as always, right on time on Monday morning, but with a palpable sense of, I thought, pity—as one opens the cage of a flightless bird. Even when her jingling and squeaking faded off into the mall, I did not rouse myself from bed. For I knew where she was heading: up to the former House of Blues, now a den of iniquity, housing as it did a murderer and usurper—a despicable creature, regardless how luxuriant and elegant, gathered as he was into that cascade of gorgeous, flowing hair.

I pictured my trip to the food court, waiting in line behind Mr. Ponytail as he demanded his morning eggs. (Poached, probably; I knew his type.) Then I'd slink up to the counter, where the teens would splat down a ladleful of yellow mush onto a paper plate, plop a teabag into some tepid water and dispatch me to my table, where Mr. Ponytail would already be situated—in my chair! What could I do but sidle up alongside him and watch as he wolfed down his eggs with aplomb? We were colleagues now, apparently, which made me complicit in all the vile, unforgivable things he'd done.

No, I would not dishonour Dennis's memory by breakfasting with his killer. Not when there was a mystery to be solved, a wrong to be righted and justice to be served. But how? I had no allies in the mall, no real agency. K. Sohail was clearly powerless. Oh, she had a good heart beneath all that beige polyester, but the mall stifled its every struggling beat. And her behaviour that morning suggested that I had indeed wounded our relationship by venturing out after dark and taking the elevator to the basement, where I'd discovered the mall's deepest, darkest secrets. (And pool.)

Lying there in bed, dragging the flaccid (despondent, I felt) tongue-hair back and forth over my teeth, I wondered what purpose I now had in the mall, what with a competitor of such magnificence and emancipating lack of morality residing upstairs. My thoughts were interrupted by a rustle in the hallway, a noise so unlikely and alien that at first I couldn't place it—even as it sharpened into voices and footsteps.

People!

I peeked out from behind my screen and there they were. Four human beings. Striding past my quarters. With purpose. With resolution. With exhilaration, I thought, my spirits deflating. I padded out to the hallway in my pyjamas to watch them turn the corner toward the food court. Toward, I knew, the escalators, and up to the second floor, where Mr. Ponytail—my rival— resided. Patrons! At this hour! Only minutes into his stint as the mall's pre-eminent resident and the dastard was already going full blazes engaging the public. No, even more disheartening: the public was engaging him. What "work" was he "making"?

I stood there, loathing myself for my curiosity, while the hair sprung to life and began to dance upon my tongue—stimulated, no doubt, by its master's unholy dominion one floor above. Yet perhaps I might find some benefit in discovering what had enticed the public with such pre-emptive fervour and commitment, and what excited my tongue-hair so. So despite myself—despite everything—I followed those four strangers up to the former House of Blues and joined the small crowd, half a dozen strong including me and an especially reverent K. Sohail, gathered outside the shop, gazing in with looks of rapture as if upon the lair of some god or demon.

Mr. Ponytail had assembled several buckets of paint along the front of the store, forming a barricade between him and his audience. He moved between them with (I thought) contrived nonchalance, a concerted (I thought) attempt to communicate his obliviousness to our presence, but which (I thought) was an obvious show of pretension. Yet it had the intended effect, turning the crowd hushed and humbled as they (*we*, I thought, with a sigh) waited for him to begin.

And so, as the hair trembled with anticipation inside my mouth, he began.

With a great flourish, Mr. Ponytail dipped himself into a bright blue number and scuttled up the wall, dragging his hindquarters like a brush. The slash of colour he left behind was striking—a cry in the dark! a wound of sky! Someone actually gasped. But then came the climax: just below the ceiling, he took a drastic turn to the left, creating what was almost a number seven (7), but not quite.

And then, like a spider, Mr. Ponytail released from the wall, dropped to the floor and lay there motionless, in a pose that was either a bow to the audience or an expression of penitence before his own work. Regardless, a clatter of applause broke out among the public, K. Sohail included; so he'd duped her too. The tongue-hair thrashed around my mouth, straining at the root with such fervour that I had to clamp my teeth to stop it from wrenching free. And, to be honest, the piece was admittedly striking, with a tantalizing tension between expectation and outcome. *What vision! What sophistication!* I fairly cried aloud, and found myself tapping hands along with everyone else.

Only when Ponytail roused himself did I remember that I was meant to loathe him. His performance was a sham, built as it was on Dennis's demise, I thought, seizing the tongue-hair between two molars and holding it fast. Regardless how exquisite his work, this guy was a reprobate. I looked around to see if anyone else was tormented by enjoying such glorious work by such an inglorious creature—but the five other faces in the hallway were aglow with a kind of benediction.

Meanwhile Ponytail seemed to have been defeated by the efforts of his own artistry. He flapped vaguely at us, his audience, as if ushering us away—*show's over*—and retreated behind his sleeping screen (an obvious upgrade from my own, replete with Eastern ornamentation of waterfalls and dragons), leaving us to stare dimly at his creation, that not-quite-seven rendered in paint the colour of a summer's day.

The four members of the public seemed to find nothing derisive in this dismissal, and in fact, if their awestruck head-shakes were any indication, were in fact impressed by it. Scorn was simply the way of the true artist—in fact, it rendered Mr. Ponytail even more compelling to his adoring public. The four of them wandered off, whispering in reverential tones—*That was something, I've never seen anything like it*, etc.—leaving me and K. Sohail alone, ten feet apart and eyeing each other awkwardly.

I ventured a nod, teeth gritted.

K. Sohail nodded back.

I sensed an opportunity. Just the two of us, a possibility for an honest exchange, maybe even the truth. But before I could speak K. Sohail placed her finger to her mouth, shushing me. She nodded toward the screen, behind which Mr. Ponytail—exhausted by his output, emotionally and physically spent—was snoring.

FOR THE REST OF THE WEEK, I faced the blank page with renewed desperation. I'd already worried that my Progress Reports, doubling as they did for "making work," were a shortcut or cheat, and now I was confronted with someone—Mr. Ponytail—whose talents were so monumental that they necessitated patricide to be set free. Would I kill for the residency? One of the teenagers at the chicken stand, perhaps? No, even they didn't deserve to die in the service of art—certainly not my "art," such as it was.

How to compete with the spectacle of Ponytail's not-quite-seven? I tried sketching an incomplete eight (8)—and realized immediately that all I'd done was write the number three (3). Fool! I'd only confirmed the guy's supremacy. He'd put his whole being into that initial piece, a literal self-impression of body, mind and spirit that altered the space irrevocably. He was his own instrument. He worked intuitively, as if channelling a transcendental communiqué from some loftier plane. He was, unfortunately, a genius.

I, meanwhile? I'd had no feedback on my Progress Reports; did K. Sohail even read them? Or were they simply passed "up the chain" to the mall's executive branch? Even then I pictured them stashed bureaucratically in a filing cabinet amid thousands of similarly ignored documents—or worse, fed straight through the shredder. My words! My *work*! Was it all for nought? Why, then, bother?

Meanwhile Mr. Ponytail's brilliance, graphically displayed upon the mall, seemed to engage the public at a fundamental level. There was no way to compete. My concerns were not the concerns of others. In fact I wasn't sure what my concerns even were. At best I spent my days trying to avoid banishment from the mall—fulfilling, in the least disruptive way possible, the requirements that permitted me to live there.

I was only occupying space, I realized, while Ponytail's activities inspired awe and delight, despite the fact that he engaged the public by treating them like swine. Was that what people wanted? To be made lesser and penitent?

It was then that I recalled, from so many weeks ago, the Ornately Hatted Woman. Yes! My first patron! Fine, my only patron. And yet. She'd liked what she'd seen. A single member of the public, which in the face of Mr. Ponytail's slavering minions might not seem like much—but still. It was a life! A human life, transformed by my work. Or at least distracted, briefly.

My god! Via my work we'd fairly fallen in love—albeit a platonic sort of love, of course, what with Klassanderella down in the islands and our wedding imminent. But compared to the public who drooled all over Mr. Ponytail, even as he slighted them, the Ornately Hatted Woman was different. She understood my work, having observed—and even inspired!—its humble beginnings and been impressed enough to return for a second look. She was a conscientious and courteous person, with clearly, if her hat was any indication, refined and particular taste; her return suggested that she saw me as the type to require space and time to really come into my own. Her absence ever since wasn't cruel, but respectful: she was simply letting me find my way.

But find my way to what?

The mall, I thought. And everything that it suffocated, trapped and concealed. All that dereliction wasn't the failure of personal enterprise; it was a symptom of something hideous and dormant, something designed to annihilate humanity itself. And I was at the cusp of discovery, which the Ornately Hatted Woman sensed, which was why she'd anointed me as her proxy. Not just my patron, then, but an ally and a muse. Unlike Mr. Ponytail, I didn't condescend to the public from on high. No, the people and I were one and the same: I was a person too! United, unified and on the side of all that was good and right—about everything.

I smiled discreetly to myself. And then, with that brand of confidence that blooms from within and flowers in an outward flush of the spirits, into the camera. Directly. Steadily. With the wild abandon of self-actualization, for a count of (almost) four. Whoever was watching—K. Sohail, the mall's powers-that-be, Dennis from the afterlife, maybe even the arrogant albeit impressive Ponytail—would witness my transformation.

No longer would I wallow in inadequacy. No longer would I be cowed by the mall. I had a purpose. I could not be stopped. The Ornately Hatted Woman would return soon enough, and I owed it to her to make her visit worthwhile. Revolution was at hand. It was time for my real work to begin.

RATHER THAN OBEDIENTLY HEADING to breakfast the following morning, I shaved my tongue (plucking the squirming hair from my razor and flushing it down the sink) and headed out of my quarters not right, but left—toward the exit and the world outside.

The world outside!

I was on a mission. And while leaving the mall might seem counterintuitive to that mission—which involved detective work *inside* the mall—I needed to reclaim some agency. To see the sky, to breathe the air, to sup, even passingly, from the trough of freedom. In my past life, I could roam (and had! oh, how I'd roamed!) the town as I pleased, save certain desolate or derelict districts where I'd be taking my life into my own hands. (A strange phrase: in whose hands was my life if not mine?)

But this was no time for semantic interrogations, I thought, striding past a long-forgotten banking-adjacent concern, Payday Cash & Loans, and an abandoned bookstore-cum-stationer, Page One Gifts. With each step I reclaimed some autonomy.

No more shuttling to the food court for my daily allotments of poultry products, like a marionette yanked along a string. I was no one's puppet. I was a human being. An animal! I was wild and free.

Yet I did worry, as I made my way down the hall, that I hadn't brought a jacket. Several weeks had passed since my internment in the mall and it seemed probable that autumn had descended. Wild animal or not, I certainly didn't want to catch a cold. And while there was no provision in my Acceptance Letter banning me from leaving the mall, anyone watching the security footage might misconstrue my little venture as a getaway. I pictured Dennis, face down in the pool—punished, clearly, but why?—and broke stride.

Coming to a halt before a former haberdashery, Impresario, Esq., I came up with a plan: if questioned, I would claim to be simply checking on my bicycle. After all, it had been chained up for weeks now, and while I had complete faith in the workday oversight of K. Sohail, there was no telling what the hooligans of our town might get up to under cover of night—a stolen brake pad here, a fecal smear there. It seemed reasonable to be concerned, especially about my only means of transportation—I was no motorist, and public transit tends to seethe with disease.

Yes: a bike check. A clever ruse indeed! Invigorated, I resumed walking past abandoned enterprises—Go-Go Snaps, Guillemot et Frère—and peered ahead for a sign of the doors to outside. Nothing yet: the view still narrowed to that distant vanishing point with failed stores lining either side. Upon my arrival at the mall, I must have been so rapt with anticipation (or dread) that I'd failed to notice its incredible size. What a hallway!

Certainly there were a lot of stores.

On and on I walked, and on and on they went, with their for-saken purposes and misbegotten futures: Sportsbarn; The Honest Dodger; Scott's Sausage; Tech Stuff; Big Bear Outfitters; Kitchen Republic; Zippy's; Pharmapause; Socrates Opticians; Biodynamic Earth Wellness Organic Foods and Fresh-Pressed Juice Bar; The Shoe Revue; Knit Knack Wool Shack; Toothworks Dentistry; Naughty Bits Adult Fun!; Kiddie Karousel Daykare; Jupiter Big and Tall Fashions for Him; Jupiter Big and Tall Fashions for Her; Nailtime; 12 to 6; Jacob Bros. Bridal Experience; TJ Lumber; Bikini Parish; Frugal & Scrounge; Dr. Duane Orthotics; EZ Play Gamez and Toyz; Golddust Jewellers; Hobby Horse Pastime Co.; Body and Soaps; Plants Forever; Tech Stuff Xpress; C'est ça?; Tech Stuff Kids; Meringue; Big Sleep Interiors; Müd.

And so on, and so on.

People, it struck me, had invested their lives in these endeav-ours. Where were they now? Bankrupted, mortified? Or had they escaped while the "getting was good" and could now be found sip-ping elaborate cocktails on a tropical isle? (*Klassanderella!*) Though all that desolation suggested more tragic fates. Like that of poor Dennis: might all these proprietors have drowned, too, in that subterranean pool? My pace slackened as I imagined the mall as a kind of beast, the basement its guts, and those crystal-clear waters the bile-flooded gut where it digested once-intrepid entrepreneurs.

Labouring now, I walked for another five minutes, or ten—with nothing to gauge my progress, it was impossible to tell how long or far I was travelling. Regardless, there was still no sign of the exit. Had I somehow gone the wrong way? Impossible; there were only two options: right to the food court, left to the outside world. And yet for hours I'd been stalking this gauntlet of broken dreams, without any end in sight.

Ten more shops went past . . . twenty, thirty . . . The names began to blur.

I stopped. My feet hurt. My legs felt weak and wobbly. My hands were swollen and fizzed slightly. The view down that interminable tunnel of deserted stores had turned vertiginous: like a shaft into, and through, the depths of hell. It was time to turn back. My worst fear was confirmed: there was no leaving the mall. At least not for me.

I DECIDED TO DEDICATE the rest of my week to scheming—
scheming, that is, under cover of "making work." With that
camera observing my quarters, I had to maintain the subterfuge
of dutifully obeying the terms of my residency. So, head down,
I set to it, while the public traipsed past, unengaged, without so
much as a glimpse my way. On their way back from the second
floor, I often overheard raving about whatever mastery Mr. Ponytail had conjured that day—*Genius! Unparalleled! Soul-edifying!*
Soul-destroying!—which provoked a little wriggle from my tongue-
hair as it surged through the flesh like a sapling; grimly I'd head
straight to the bathroom and hack it down to size.

The problem, however, was that "making work" took up so
much of my time (50%) and energy (100%) that no scheme
materialized. It merely itched at the back of my mind like a hair
upon the tongue. Each night I went to bed harbouring instincts
of mutiny, but these didn't develop beyond a vague aspiration,
which itself felt feeble and misguided. I quite liked the phrase
Vengeance is mine, for example, but when I tried to picture myself

uttering it, all I could summon was an image of a doleful figure hunched over a desk, scribbling away: hardly the stuff of glory.

Also K. Sohail's nightly send-offs had begun to sound hollow, as if gutted from within. Each *goodnight* no longer had the melancholy ring of communion between a lonely keeper and her lonelier keep, and I no longer felt eased by her words into sleep, but repelled from the living world into one of vague, colourless dreams. A wall had grown between us: one constructed by Mr. Ponytail, yes, but more so it was the wall of the mall. Each of us trapped on our respective sides, in our respective roles. How to tear it down? How to set us both free, and escape?

Meanwhile more and more people were flooding in from the outside world to experience Mr. Ponytail's incomparable "work." By the end of the week, even the food court was bustling, with some three dozen people spaced around the tables and a line six deep at the chicken stall. The teenagers behind the counter worked feverishly. One impaled pale raw birds on skewers, another tonged their bronzed and blistering counterparts free, which a third hacked to bits and served, while a fourth took orders and stuffed the till with cash.

I stood at the periphery of the food court, observing the crowd. The way Ponytail's toadies feasted had the ring of celebration, of avowal and tribute. This wasn't just lunch: it was a kind of banquet. In Ponytail's honour. Legs of chicken were lofted in salute. Iced teas were raised in toasts. Smoke from the grill wafted up to the rafters in a kind of greasy mist. Repugnant, all of it! What had once been my twice-daily personal domain had been reduced to this sick bonanza. As the food court's sole and dedicated customer—save that couple who'd bequeathed me my ring (which now I furtively pocketed, afraid the "rightful owner" might be among these masses) and my ill-fated comrade Dennis—I'd enjoyed special treatment, bordering on veneration, from the chicken teens. My regular order was delivered swiftly with a deferential bow. I no longer needed to produce my Acceptance Letter. They knew me. I had become a figure of towering importance in the mall, or at least in the food court at appointed meal times.

But now? Now I stood at the edge of it all like a fool toeing the shoreline while a great orgy of lecherous bathers frolicked and romped through the surf. If I wanted lunch I'd have to line up for it among these plebeian masses—a great lost tribe dedicated to the veneration of my enemy. Fans, acolytes. Disciples, even, of someone who was at best an impostor and at worst a murderer. Whom did I have? Klassanderella, sure, but she was hundreds of miles away . . .

Suddenly the clucking of conversation was interrupted by cheers that went roaring around the room. And then they were all standing and clapping and chanting his name in a sort of frenzied call-and-response:

MIS-ter! Pony-TAIL!

MIS-ter! Pony-TAIL!

I shrunk behind a pillar.

After a few rounds, the deranged lot of them sat, chortling at a job well done, and a round of cheers rippled through the room: plastic cups were tapped; iced tea was chugged.

I scanned the crowd for the Ornately Hatted Woman. No sign of her: in absentia, she maintained her devotion to me. Though the support of my only patron might have bolstered my sagging spirits, I had to trust that the Ornately Hatted Woman would loyally return for my "piece of resistance" . . . whatever that might be. Not "work," certainly; I couldn't imagine even my Final Report passing any sort of professional muster. I would have to produce something far more revelatory, a grand disclosure of the mall's nefarious secrets . . . But how? Some type of banner? Where would I get the materials?

Though my stomach was rumbling, I couldn't bring myself to enter this mindless, puerile throng, none of whom even glanced my way. Surely they were aware of the mall's original resident. What cruelty not to seek me out, even as a show of politesse. A cursory glance into my quarters, a nod of recognition. It wouldn't take much. They walked right past me! Was I really so inept and my activities—my "work"—so insipid as not to warrant even the most basic acknowledgement?

Heading back to my quarters, suffering a hunger as profound as any I'd ever known, my alienation flared into rage. Ponytail's minions weren't just misguided and rude and literally "eating my lunch," they were imbeciles. Enticed by inane spectacle and cowed by parlour tricks. They were slaves to mob rule, caught up in the spectacle of a fraudulent megalomaniac slashing not-quite-sevens up the walls. Impressive, sure. But not *visionary*. Mr. Ponytail didn't care about his audience; he only had eyes for himself.

Well, I had seen things.

And I would show these people. I would show them all.

PROGRESS REPORT #5

It's hard to imagine a greater tribute than a banquet in your honour. Not simply a gathering of devotees supplicating before your majesty, but one with a compulsory feasting aspect too. A banquet isn't any old meal. No, multiple "services" culminate with a whole animal broiled in its living skin and presented as such, trotters and all, with a fruit crammed in its maw. Is the fruit forbidden? Kind of. It's there mostly for camouflage, unappetizing as it can be to chew on something's thigh with a full view of its face.

What a banquet is, is an orgy of food. And a banquet specifically for you is an orgy with you as its auteur, directing bodies into whichever formulation strikes your fancy. Or else simply lying back and accommodating this chap or gal's escalations of pleasure. "Let's have at it," you might say, pointing at a bowl of succulent mutton or rutabaga stew. And then you make love to it with your mouth amid thunderous cheers all around.

Other than a sow or billy, what other dishes might be on offer? All the classics. Before dinner even begins, one entrées with the spoils of the orient: figs, olives, capers, nectarines, dates, mixed nuts, rices, raisins, sundry items cured and curried, "delight," etc. You appreciate the gesture, and normally you'd join the masses gorging like jackals upon a fresh, gut-frothing corpse, but tonight you're above the free-for-all. Tonight you're above everything.

After a while, someone hurls a glass to the floor and screams the name of their favourite grandparent. It's the signal to sit. Everyone waits for you to take your seat first, standing around awkwardly with their hands perched on their chair backs. What nervous birds! And you taunt them, don't you. Crouching halfway, then rocketing to your feet, then wandering around for a bit, before finally racing to your throne and assuming it like the grand monarch you are—tonight, anyway.

The banquet opens with bread rolls, crusty on the outside and the opposite within, and freshly churned butter ripe for the slathering. There's (grape) wine by the gallon, as rich and purple as wet liver and twice as sweet.

The first course is a steaming bisque, sprinkled adoringly with salts dredged from a nearby seabed. It's delicious. Then more rolls and more butter (in constant supply; no one can get enough), and a slice of cheese each, for everyone.

What's next? A salad as green as the hills. The vinaigrette is to die for. Nobody dies, though, not tonight—no one would dare ruin your evening. The leaves of the salad are impervious to the dressing's moisture and remain crisp until the final vegetal shred.

Then a snack to "amuse the mouth," something exquisite spiralled upon a cracker. Caviar, probably. You munch it down, offering your compliments to the chef. But the chef won't hear it, for tonight the only one worthy of praise is you. "I'm human garbage," she calls from the kitchen, hanging her head in shame, "actually."

That's right, no singing for your supper! Instead everyone else sings for you. "He or she's a jolly good fellow or ma'am," they sing, and laugh, and you laugh too, and shrug, and guzzle your flagon. There are shields on the wall, and swords, and in the fireplace roars a mighty conflagration. You're right at the head of the table, the lord or lady-lord of dinner. Yet benevolent, certainly. It's not like you're forbidding the lesser attendees from eating, or spearing your neighbour with a fork.

Here's the next course: veal. It's so young and tender you can fairly hear it bawling, and the blood gushes forth with every bite. Wow.

Then some sausages.

Then vegetables in blond sauce.

Then a hen.

Then a whole marlin, spike to tail.

Then a classic goulash of potato, egg, lentil and bean.

Then a "mystery meat." (Ibis? No one knows.)

Then another hen, i.e., *hen two ways*.

Then a sort of froth.

Then a slice of melon and two almonds, arranged in a smile.

Then a break for speeches. These follow one after the next, with titles like "Were I Not So Lesser?" and "Ne'er a Clout Deservéd" and "Praise Be the Abundant One!" Maybe there's even a moment of silence, suggested by one of the more distinguished and ornately hatted speakers. Words can't capture your grandeur, she concedes, and crawls under the table in shame. So for a full minute everyone just shuts their mouth and stares at you, unblinking, and you stare back. Pretty soon they're all crying. Not too shabby!

Then a spaghetti.

Then two fondues.

Then an assembly of fricasseed leaves, cuke spears and artfully shaven radish.

Then "wings."

Then a palate-cleansing beet.

Then—my god—*another hen*!

Then gravy, served almost tenderly in a carafe. It steams in the middle of the table like the orifices of one's snowbound beloved.

A pause.

What's to be done? Go at it with a straw?

A rumour circulates that this gravy has been sapped from the main course, which is gusting great wafts of its enchanting odour from the kitchen. The smell is enough to re-whet even the most vomitously sated appetite, and it hurls the guests into fits of rapture—for more food, but also at the possibility of clinging a little longer to your company.

The gossip mill speaks the truth: here it is, the main event, a great sizzling carcass wheeled out on a trolley. What a huge animal, too, and fresh, having been shot in the head first thing that morning. And it's all just for you.

While you devour the beast, everyone chants your name. They'd love a taste, of course, but they're glad to merely bear witness. You're a shining light, a beacon of hope, a spark of grace in the interminable darkness of their dismal, meaningless lives.

How is it? Sumptuous, naturally. The skin is just right. And the meat? Let's just say you've rarely chewed anything so juicy. And it's just for you—the whole thing, mane and all, right down to the gleaming hooves.

Then at the end they give you a plaque.

TWO

WHEN PREVIOUSLY I'D ONLY BEEN SCHEMING about how to scheme without getting caught, I spent the entire next week actually scheming in earnest.

Inspired by the virtue of Klassanderella, the patronage of the ornately hatted woman, the potential vindication of Dennis's murder, the possibility of trouncing the depraved Ponytail and his disciples and freeing K. Sohail and myself from the mall, trapped as we were within its tyrannical regime, I schemed. Oh, how I schemed! And after several days of said scheming I had schemed a scheme so brilliant, so cunning, so unexpected (especially to myself) that, glutted with nerve, I dared to utter my favourite phrase . . .

Vengeance is mine, I whispered into the shadows. Or if not quite "whispered," exactly, then mouthed, or at the least very loudly thought.

Whether my catchphrase was spoken aloud or not was irrelevant. As the mall shut down for the day, a surge of heat flushed from my loins up into the face and went sparkling down through my limbs: the spirit glitter of rebellion.

I watched the chicken teens clear out and the last of Ponytail's followers drift back to their sad and empty lives. That others were permitted to come and go from the mall didn't bother me. My body thrummed with imminent glory. Soon enough I would prove that good could triumph over evil—if I didn't qualify as "good," exactly, I was certainly too ineffectual to be considered "evil," which seemed to require a lot of effort, not to mention a capacity for homicide.

At any rate, the stakes were high.

The lights dimmed. On came the security lanterns. K. Sohail's signature jingle and squeak echoed faintly from somewhere off in the mall. And as she approached, that revolutionary sparkle curdled into a hot gnarl of disquiet in my gut.

But this was no time for bowel movements. The moment of action was at hand.

It was time.

Instead of waiting in bed, I greeted K. Sohail at the gate, preempting her usual bromides by asking what Mr. Ponytail had accomplished that afternoon; I'd been busy "making work," I explained, and was sad to have missed the exhibition. K. Sohail flushed visibly, turning shy and discombobulated. After a few halting starts at summarizing the day's masterpiece, she shook her head, shuffled from one foot to the other, lapsed into silence and finally offered a chastened and helpless shrug.

The desired effect! Humbling K. Sohail might have been cruel—but it was necessary. Shamed by her feeble attempts to capture the great artist's virtuosity, sheepishly she withdrew, nearly tripping over her feet as she backed away. Goodnight, I said commandingly. K. Sohail bowed in apology—not to me, of course, but to the legacy of Mr. Ponytail—and scurried off down the hallway without so much as a reply.

For once I didn't need that sweet send-off; my scheme was afoot. I listened until the caretaker's retreat faded completely. Satisfied that she was gone, I slipped from my unlocked quarters into the dim blue light and headed to the food court.

I had work to do. Actual *work*, too, and not the arbitrary busy-work that one "made"; what lay ahead wasn't token fabrication of content to fill some illusory container, but a meaningful task that required moxie and valour. Fortunately I had my ring back on, and my House of Blues (Dennis, R.I.P.) jeans were really starting to come into their own; after several days of uninterrupted wear, they had moulded to my legs like a second, denim skin.

Every night the chicken teens dutifully cleaned the stall, wiped down the counters, dismantled and scoured the grill, and replaced the stainless steel skewers in the rack for the next day's trade. As I entered the food court, these skewers glistened in the pale moon-glow permitted by the skylight. I hopped the counter and slid one free: about the length of a walking cane and sharpened to deadly points at both ends. But could it impale a foe?

I swung the thing sword-like through the air, jabbing, feinting, lunging, parrying an imaginary attack—and then plunging in for the kill. A slash to the throat, a stab to the eye, and then, with my make-believe rival driven to his knees, I took my weapon by the hilt and plunged it through his spine and out through his stomach, pinning him to the tiles. Next I gored his bowels, stirring them like a soup, before scooping everything free—a spleen, a liver, some sort of glandular arrangement, the whole lot, lined up along my skewer like a kebab—only to slurp from the tip each organ, one by one, and swallow it all down in glorious, cannibalistic triumph. (Imagined, of course.)

Yes. The chicken skewer would do nicely.

Next was armour: food trays wedged up the front and back of my shirt, and an oversized napkin container emptied of its contents and donned as a helmet, with the slot providing a vertical visor. The napkins I stuffed inside my jeans, trusting that the padding wouldn't compromise their exquisite shape. Still, if anyone tried to bite my shins, they would feast on paper.

Satisfactorily carapaced, I headed to the service elevator and closed myself in.

With the mystery button illuminated, the thing chugged to life. I prepared myself for the lengthy voyage ahead and leaned against the wall with my spear at my side. (My armour didn't permit me to sit down.) But no sooner had the elevator begun moving than it shuddered to a stop. Busted? Out of operation? Or had I arrived at the pool already?

I cracked the doors and squinted through the gap in my helmet. Instead of the claustrophobic glare of the white-tiled hallway, I was greeted by shadows and a musty smell of mildew and gasoline. I hauled the doors open all the way. This wasn't the pool level at all. The elevator had brought me to a different place altogether: an underground parking garage. And somewhere, off in the distance, music was playing.

As someone who had (and still has) never driven a car, the space of the parking garage was alien to me. Were they usually soundtracked? I'd never had cause to visit one; they lurked beneath the institutions of our town (the library, the hospital, the "bureau") like each building's subconscious—unknowable, unseen, unimaginable. What went on down there? Parking, ostensibly, which one could only trust proceeded under humane conditions. Better to hope that a resurfacing motorist was among the majority—not some lucky survivor.

But who was I to say? Perhaps, being one storey closer to hell, they hosted accordingly depraved activities. Did one gut it out against other drivers for "spots," with victory arriving from great flaming wrecks, unspeakable injuries to person and property, the odd fatality? Likely not, I'd always reasoned, having faith in the basic protocols of civilization and traffic. Still, I was happy to travel by bicycle, limited only by the objects to which it could be chained.

At any rate. I was in one now, and the parking garage was not what I'd imagined! No one was *parking*, for example; everyone was already parked, with hundreds of cars lined up precisely in endless rows. The lighting, too, was odd: a green wash, like the mall but swampier. Everything was so still. And, save the far-off music, so silent. Nowhere had I ever experienced such a simultaneous sense of infinitude and claustrophobia.

I'd anticipated something a little more cavernous, down here below the earth's crust. But this was so *close*. Regularly spaced pillars propped up the low ceiling—and everything above, I realized with awe. Though this would have been even more extraordinary in the mall's more prosperous days, what with the mobs of shoppers prowling the stores, I still marvelled at such a feat of engineering. At the hubris of it, really. To think that a space could be hollowed out *underneath a building* where people might abandon their cars, which they'd then *walk atop* like angels or kings!

My napkin-dispenser helmet was obstructing my vision, so I removed it—trusting that nothing would come hurtling from the dark and knock me on the noggin. I'd never seen so many cars. Not just hundreds, possibly thousands. Parked side by each with an aisle down the middle, on and on. So eerily motionless—almost dormant. Whose were they? Surely not only Mr. Ponytail's adoring public; there were too many for that. Who, then, had left their cars here, and where had they gone?

And what of the music? Was a soundtrack common to parking garages? Something to accompany motorists back to their vehicles, a jaunty tune to put a bounce in one's step and a jangle in one's keys? But then, I thought, that sort of music would surely be "piped in." This music seemed to generate from a location far off in the parking garage, played specifically and vibrantly by, I was convinced, a "live" musician.

Someone was out there. Or, I thought, someones: I could make out several instruments twining together. Though, I thought, such a thing could be the work of one of those crafty talents who strap a drum to their back and trumpets to their feet and so on, a human orchestra deploying every physical tool at their disposal, from mouth to fingers to sheer will, thrashing around percussively while blowing and strumming melodies and harmonies and counter-melodies and god knows what else.

The shambolic unity of the music—ragged and wild and almost frantic, yet cohesively so—confirmed it: this was the work of a so-called "one man or woman band."

Here was a true talent, a real artist—not like Mr. Ponytail with all his braggadocio and self-aggrandizing theatrics. How I wished Ponytail's duped minions might learn from this expression of tremendous personal dignity—of hope and of joy, but of struggle too. Their master was a charlatan, they'd realize after only a few bars; the music of the parking garage was "the real deal." What integrity this person must have, I thought, performing to no audience, yet still trying to reach something elemental through song. For the simple pleasure of making music. For the soul!

I felt a surge of aspirational kinship: this music expressed something about me too. I had to meet its creator. And so I set aside my revolutionary scheme and skewer-spear for a moment, stepped from the elevator in my ersatz body armour, and trundled into the parking garage, food trays clacking, toward whoever was tootling on whatever horn or wind, twanging strings, "tickling the ivories"—who knew; I was no expert.

To be honest, I had no ear for music at all. In fact, after being diagnosed as a tone-deaf youngster, my role in our school choir had been to stand by our conductor and turn the pages of her sheet music. Ever since, I'd been resistant to songs of any sort, which tended to ignite a pain-memory of paper cuts—my fingertips lacerated by the scores of various operettas, carols, shanties and spirituals, blood streaming down my shirtsleeves while my classmates belted outs their hearts.

Yet this music struck me with a poignancy I'd never known. It didn't make me feel bad; in fact . . . dare I say *good*? (Certainly curious.) That sweet, sad song wafted almost vaporously—like curling tendrils of smoke, like beckoning fingers—through the parking garage. The instrumentation was warm, welcoming. It lulled and summoned. It seemed not just to reach me, I felt, but to be reaching *for* me. To embrace and pull me in. Whoever played this music really "had my number." And their song called me, sirenlike, with warmth and grace. At least so I hoped, and not to lure me through the parking garage to my brutal, grisly death.

I pushed into the aisle between cars that, in their almost meditative stillness, seemed to be awaiting reanimation. Like creatures asleep. To avoid waking them I crept along furtively— which, because of my armour, was an awkward, almost sultry manoeuvre between a tiptoe and a lurch—while the music echoed through the parking garage. Like the love song of a ghost, I thought. Or a lullaby hummed dolefully to oneself, if one could sing oneself to sleep. Could one? Unclear; I'd never tried.

What music, I thought, creeping toward it between the cars. So melancholy and sweet. Lilting up, cascading down. Here a trill, there a flutter. The rhythm knocked like a pulse, as if the song itself was a living thing. Yet despite that steady beat, the melody shifted through moods. Whose moods? Mine, somehow. But also its creator's, as if we shared a consciousness, maybe even a past. If the song had a name it was "Us." My god, who was responsible for such beauty? Such insight! Such acuity!

On I walked, occasionally adjusting my food-tray breastplate, toward, I felt, some undiscovered part of myself.

But was the music getting any closer? Hard to say. As with my failed escape from the mall, it was impossible to gauge my progress along that uniform channel between cars. With everything washed in that sickly green light, limiting colour to varying shades of darkness, I couldn't tell a blue car from a red—never mind a maroon from a burgundy. And the gobbledygook of the licence plates was even less helpful than the names of the shops, which were at least identifiably different, not to mention legible, words.

That said, every now and then I did glimpse a "personal" plate, featuring some odd combination of letters and numbers encrypted into a slogan or epithet (BOY IDER, I DOMN8, 2GUD4U, etc.) These flashes of ego would have provided helpful signposts amid all that anonymity if their arrogance weren't so generic and uniform. Never mind that such vanity was completely antithetical to the humble, human music of the parking garage, which drifted through the greenish glow like the enticing scent of a lovingly cooked meal—crafted and presented, I was certain, by a genius.

Sure, I was taking a momentary self-involved diversion from avenging Dennis's murder, and perhaps delaying my takedown of the mall in the process, but meeting the musician responsible for a work of such profound artistic clarity seemed essential to my mission—perhaps I'd even been summoned there by metaphysical means. Knowing that I had a kindred spirit in the mall was already invigorating; maybe when we met my quest would inspire this sir or madam to pack up their kit and join me. An ally, imagine. And a soundtrack for the revolution!

The armour, it struck me, was a mistake: not the costume of camaraderie but one of suspicion. So I shed the trays and unpacked the napkins from my jeans, leaving them in a neat little pile on the hood of some sedan. On I crept with new agility, lithe as a leopard. I began peering past the windshields—every car was facing out, having been "backed in"—in case a human being sat behind the wheel. But there was no sign of drivers or passengers. The cars began to strike me as awaiting not just reanimation but their maiden voyage, as if the entire fleet was on standby until some command summoned it to life.

No sooner had I formed this thought, the cars came on with a roar.

All of them. Thousands of engines from one end of the parking garage to the other coughed and turned over and revved furiously, and their blazing headlights spotlit the lane from both sides. Like a stage. With me upon it, paralyzed in the glare.

Abandoning my armour suddenly felt foolish. Had the cars been waiting for me to let down my guard? With no protection, I could easily be pulverized. Yet for now they simply idled, their lights cast over me, their engines beastly and ravenous, the odour of burning gasoline choking the air.

I listened amid it all for the music—even a distant tremor of that beautiful song—off somewhere in the parking garage.

Nothing. Only cars.

Looking down the aisle I noticed a distant blurring at the— for lack of a better word—horizon, way down at the end of the parking garage. The blurring seemed to be . . . getting closer. I squinted. Yes, definitely, something was smudging the illuminated area between the cars.

And as it came ever closer, I realized what was happening. Nothing was approaching. The cars were simply nudging forward so that their noses touched, two by two, in a sort of wave, snuffing out their lights into a faint sliver between fenders. Closer and closer surged this darkness—which, when it reached me, I realized with horror, would sever me in half at the waist.

What else to do? I turned and ran. Away from the dimming light, past my armour on the hood of that grumbling sedan—no time to grab it! I kept running, glancing back over my shoulder at the cars pulling together behind me, one and then the next, closer and closer down the line: a rev of engines, a lurch forward, a screech of brakes, their lights reduced to a faint glow between their fenders.

The safety of the elevator was almost in reach. But the colliding cars, too, were nipping at my heels. I could feel their shadow approaching: a coolness on the back of my neck, a chill in my heart. Another twenty yards—fifteen!—ten!

I was readying myself to dive inside the elevator when I felt something bump against my legs—almost gently. And when I tried to take another step, I could not. I struggled. To no avail.

The cars had caught me.

I'd not been halved—preferable!—but I was still trapped, with two fenders pinching me snugly just below the knee. I watched as the four remaining cars ahead of me pulled together as well. In both directions the cars had now completely closed in, cuddled up nose to nose, headlights kissing. And me pinned, with the elevator only steps away.

Everything returned to stillness.

The cars' engines died.

Their lights extinguished too.

Silence.

Except, no: from far off in the parking garage once again came that music. Lovely and still seductive, though maybe rueful now too.

Had I been tricked? Or had the cars, working for the mall, merely recognized that I'd found my spiritual other and thwarted my journey?

I squirmed, kicked, flailed. Useless. I stooped, panting. And listened with a heavy heart to that faraway song—as beautiful as ever. But then guilt flooded in alongside the music. Here was someone "making work" while I stood uselessly about like some sort of potted plant. The least I could do with this moment of stasis was *use it*. So I set to mentally sketching a Progress Report to recast the current situation as one of jubilation and glory. I would show the mall that my spirits wouldn't be dampened!

A first line struck me—*For those blessed with bipedal function, there's nothing quite like a walk.*—and it went from there:

And not just walking: no, the indefinite article is paramount. A walk is an entity, an ontology, an existence. Walking is mere transportation—functional, generic and deficient in mystery, as the vagary of "murdering" lacks the exhilarating specificity and intrigue of "a murder." And of course "the walk" almost always implies "to the gallows," the worst walk of all.

What else is not a walk? Pacing, for one—that's the anxious fretting about of a madman or -woman, a twitchy mind transmuted into manic action. Back and forth, back and forth. Like a malfunctioning cuckoo plunging from his clock to proclaim some erroneous hour, retreating, then bursting forth again, goggle-eyed with madness—shrieking, thrusting, shrieking.

Stalking suggests the vampiric and predatory. A weird-angled lean of the torso, a daft glaze in the eyes, the jaw slightly ajar, a thread of drool dangling from the chin. Stalkers ply their trade down by the canal, or in a ditch. It's that shameful and gross. One would never proudly announce, "I'm off for a stalk!" No, stalking is too suspicious, too criminal, too embarrassing, the province of lackeys, organ pirates and the pathologically deranged.

A stroll is too leisurely, almost lackadaisical; invariably you'll trip. Sauntering is arrogant; promenading pretentious; marching militaristic. One can only amble about the hills and dales—try it in the city, get creamed by a bus. Those who wander are harmless enough but will inevitably—and irritatingly—require rescue. To mosey implies a voyeuristic subterfuge: one "moseys on over to this window to have a look-see," i.e., to watch a stranger remove his pants. Snoops mosey. Creeps too. It's one step from slinking! (Which one performs only in the dead of night, slathered in grease.)

No, give me a walk any day of the week. Monday, for example. Or Boxing Day, etc. One dons a comfy pair of walking shoes, selects a robust walking stick from the woodpile, adjusts one's walking hat to a jaunty tilt and hits the streets. The slap of footfalls on pavement is the sweetest music on earth. You swing your arms, you glance this way and that. With your feet providing the beat, a nearby bird trills a delightful tune: tweedle-dee-dum, diggity-doo-dah, poopity-glee! Life is as sweet as a plum sucked straight from the branch—when you're on a walk, that is. Rarely otherwise.

Who else is about? An amputee looking on enviously from his haunches. A baby thinking, "Someday . . ." And maybe a fellow walker passing in the opposite direction who, admiring your gait, offers a collegial nod. Do you return it? Sure. But mostly out of duty. Her walk is kind of strange.

Where does a walk lead you? It doesn't matter. That's the point. Though not as mindless as wandering (see above), a walk isn't the pursuit of some endpoint or goal. Your destination is the journey, your journey the destination; there is no destination. That said, a circuit is ideal, lest you find yourself stranded atop a hillock or tunnelling into the earth's molten core.

In times like these—the end times, that is—it's more important than ever not to get caught racing the human rats of this so-called civilization. You see them zip past at a clip, off to some rendezvous or function in a power suit and/or chaps. Walking, sure—putting one foot forward, then the next, propelling off the back heel, etc. Their technique is flawless. But still, they don't "get it," lost as they are to themselves and their own, putrid hearts.

Who does get it? You do, of course. Or anyone, really, with legs and feet and a soul who synchronizes all three in harmony to roam their city's streets.

Why? Because it's pure being. Nothing to lose, nothing to gain. Walking's a zero-sum affair, and what's better than that?

Why, a walk, that's what. The thrust of this missive.

Where? Anywhere you please.

When? Same answer.

How? There is no how. Not really. Simply open the door, believe in yourself for once in your godforsaken life, step out into the world and go.

A fine ending.

And, overall, as adequate a Progress Report as any I'd written—crafted entirely in my thoughts! I couldn't wait to write it up and hand it over to K. Sohail with aplomb. Whether she read it or not, this was undoubtedly the best work I'd made yet.

Though as I began to trace back over certain phrases, that initial satisfaction ceded to melancholy. The pain behind them felt, this time, a little too acute. The whole thing rang with the fragility of overcompensation and trembled with loss. This Progress Report was far too transparently the work of one who *could not walk*— who was trapped in a "sticky situation" with no way out.

I gazed down at my legs, wedged between the fenders of a station wagon and a coupe. Held fast, I was going nowhere fast.

I have heard, at various occasions in my life, the term "pain tolerance." Apparently human suffering rates on a scale, with 1 connoting the sort of benign, almost negligible discomfort that one has to be reminded to feel, and 10 being equivalent to agony so tortuous that death seems preferable. At one end of the spectrum would be a crick in the neck, and at the other something like finding oneself stuffed in a vat of flammable acid and simultaneously drowning, suffocating, dissolving and being burned alive, or, as another example, having one's face chewed off by a blunt-toothed mule.

I am not sure where being wedged between cars in a parking garage rates on this scale. A six? Was the scale subjective and personal, or had some agreed-upon baseline been established? But how was that fair to, say, a baby, who bawls at a shift in the wind? It seemed absurd to measure an infant's "pain tolerance" alongside those lunatics at the circus who willingly pierce their own flesh with swords, or a bearded adventurer who ascends arctic glaciers until his toes turn blue and fall off—and *keeps going*.

Certainly anyone would have found my predicament uncomfortable. And the way in which my legs were stuck, with a slight twist at the knee, ached in a way that was already making me sweat. Was this how it would end, I thought: in a parking garage? No! Even I didn't deserve such an ignominious fate. I glanced around for something with which to saw my legs off—half-heartedly, I'll admit, as even just cutting my daily chicken gave me the heebie-jeebies. The idea of hacking through my own flesh might have been appealing in the abstract—in the distant abstract, viz. the eventual freedom—but the notion of positioning a saw or blade or shard of glass above my thigh was enough to make me reconsider.

No, amputation wasn't likely. What other options did I have? Screaming, obviously.

After ninety seconds of that, I gave up. My throat felt like I'd scraped it out with a trowel. Besides, my screams drowned out the music, which was, at this point, all I had to live for. And I am not being hyperbolic. If I were to suffer a slow death in the parking garage, either by starvation or some thrombotic, gangrenous ailment, at least I had a beautiful soundtrack—even if said soundtrack was the reason I found myself in this predicament in the first place. Which is not to say that I was convinced that the musician, way off in the parking garage, was in cahoots with the cars.

Or were they?

And here the real trouble began: I began to speculate.

My thoughts drifted from accountability to motivation. Never mind who had trapped me here, I thought—what was more compelling was *why*? It made no sense, I reasoned, for cars to clutch a human for the thrill of it. Was my incapacitation so thrilling? My humiliation? Perhaps. Certainly childhood had taught me the joy of a good prank. For example, being forced to eat a rose, thorns and all, by a playground bully—what laughs we had, the whole school in hysterics as I choked down every last, bitter petal. Teachers too.

But then I began to consider that the cars' renewed dormancy suggested only the first stage of some grander scheme. They seemed again to be waiting for something.

Spiders?

God. Was this merely some sort of auto web ensnaring me for its eight-legged master's supper? I peered into the gloom of the parking garage to see if anyone or anything was on its way. Though maybe not a spider . . . It would have to be very organized, and very big. More likely a human maniac. An unhinged mechanic, maybe, who'd outfitted an armada of vehicles with a trapping feature to serve her cannibalistic appetites. Or perhaps I wouldn't even be eaten. Perhaps it was worse—experiments, say, or torture. What if a whole coven of weirdos lived down here in the parking garage—the drivers of the cars, maybe. Weirdos by the thousands! Maybe they were hiding in the cars even now, awaiting their order or the "witching hour" when they'd emerge in their shrouds to scamper about and summon whatever demon they worshipped via the ritualistic disembowelment of yours truly.

Something was reading my mind. Because *right then* the music went silent and all the trunks of the cars unlocked with a great echo of clunky clicks and wheezed open.

The lids gaped at haphazard angles. For a moment everything went still.

What now? What would emerge? Spiders? Weirdos? Or vampires! Yes: this was their crypt, each car's trunk a sarcophagus. But what did crawl out of the darkness was far more horrifying than spiders or weirdos, or even men. No, what climbed from the cars in a great, dark wave of malevolence and pure, seething evil was something so foul even my wildest nightmares could never have imagined it . . .

PONYTAILS.

PONYTAILS BY THE DOZENS, by the hundreds, by the thousands—and beyond!

A veritable nation of ponytails, slithering out of the trunks, over the cars and onto the hoods, where they all perched for a moment in the dim green light. The closest specimen, a few feet away, seemed to regard me with curiosity, swaying this way and that. There was something infantile about it, as if the thing were just hatched and discovering the world for the first time.

The trunks slammed shut with a uniform clunk that resounded through the parking garage like thunder. On my tongue I felt a familiar stirring as the hair roused itself to join its unholy brethren. I tried stifling the thing against the roof of my mouth, yet I still felt it squirm. Meanwhile the ponytails rose up on their hindquarters like a legion of silky cobras poised to strike.

Had I stumbled on some sort of diabolical nursery? Who knew what their master, up there in the mall, might have planned for his disgusting army. I'd suspected that his "work" was merely a devious ruse. (Imagine his Progress Reports—pages of lies!) But

I'd never guessed the horrific scope of what he was building down here. Without taking my eyes off the nearest ponytail, I wriggled but still couldn't get free, while the hair inside my tongue was dancing to break loose—to join them.

But the ponytails just stretched, twisted and nestled down into little spirals; they seemed to be sleeping. Whether to rest or to gather themselves for a full-fledged attack, I couldn't say. And in a kind of wicked sympathy, my legs were falling asleep too: a numbing fizz crept up my calves as if the blood were carbonating. The first signs of atrophy? Perhaps my lower legs would wither and fall off, allowing me to shuffle to freedom on a pair of stumps. But how long would *that* take, I wondered, eyeing the ponytails nervously.

We waited like this, at an impasse, for some time: me trapped, my tongue-hair writhing, the ponytails slumbering. Were I to perish down here, in the parking garage, how fitting and perverse that it would be either enacted (if they ate me) or witnessed (if I starved to death on their watch) by the progeny, or at least relatives, of my nemesis. No rebellion, no liberation—no wedding to Klassanderella on the sparkling sands of her native isle. I gazed forlornly down at my engagement ring. What folly, what hubris, to try to project one's future . . .

How I loathed Mr. Ponytail then, and loathed his entire species! They were all "cut from the same cloth"—not the "cloth" of Dennis's head, exactly, but a generic cloth of despicability. I shifted my gaze hatefully to the nearest specimen, curled up in blithe repose upon the hood of a station wagon. A monster, just like its homicidal overlord.

No sooner had I thought this than the ponytails shot up, en

masse—convincing me they were reading my mind. So I tried a different tack: *I love ponytails*, I thought, as emphatically as possible. *The ponytail is my favourite species on earth!*

This failed to stall their movements. As one, thousands of ponytails went slithering down the hoods of the cars and disappeared between the fenders with a rustling, whispery sound, and then began twining into one giant mass.

I froze.

The noise quieted.

My tongue-hair went still. Everything went still.

And then, in a great tsunami of bristling hair, they came: streaming between the cars. Coming for me.

I screamed, thrashed, was held fast at the knees. The single hair in my mouth used this sudden freedom to burst through the flesh of my tongue, two inches long now and dancing in celebration against my teeth.

The whispering became a roar. In a great flood and with the thunder of surf, the ponytails—or was it now one massive ponytail?—fell upon me. My deadened feet were submerged under a carpet of hair. I closed my eyes and tensed, heart pounding, for their faceward creep up my legs and torso to join the hair in my mouth, and for the whole diabolical lot of them to pour through my body as they had in my nightmares. To consume and destroy me.

Instead they came no higher than my ankles, like a pair of tennis socks.

And continued past to the elevator.

Well. So the ponytails had somewhere to be, apparently, and were ignoring me completely. My tongue-hair slumped—forlorn, forsaken. And for a moment, watching them flow like a mischief of rats not into the waiting car but past it, up into the shaft—and beyond—I felt rejected, too, and envious. Such purpose! Such unity! Where were they off to? The mall, to meet their literal maker? Or down to another, lower level on some demonic mission?

The last of the ponytails slipped past me into the elevator shaft and out of sight. Their roaring quieted. The garage was empty again. As if on cue, the cars eased silently back into place. And so, almost anticlimactically, I was released. I shook out my legs. Numb, but functional.

And then, as if to taunt me, the music started again, way off in the parking garage. I found myself leaning toward it—but no. I wouldn't again fall prey to its seductions, not after this ordeal. Who knew what was next: the cars might turn carnivorous and devour me, or perhaps they'd birth a squadron of some even more fiendish hairstyle.

I took a moment to enjoy the music, and the fact that the instrumentalist had survived the onslaught of cars and ponytails. And while the first step of my insurrection had been something of a nonstarter, perhaps simply hearing that remarkable song was its own reward. And now, I thought, turning at last and making my way to the elevator, it was time to go. I had revenge to reap!

But first, I had to return to my quarters to log the week's Progress Report—something better than the enervated, feeble attempt I'd concocted in my head. Less pained, less compensatory. Whatever it would be, I had to maintain an illusion of compliance: not only "making work," per the protocols of my residency, but work that would seem bright-eyed and carefree, and not tarnished with loss. No, my goal was not personal revelation but to lull the mall into complacency while I marshalled my forces and wits and prepared to strike—like the mongoose as it seized the ponytail-shaped cobra by the throat and chomped right through to its bitter, snaky bones.

PROGRESS REPORT #6

Of all the mechanized joys available, few are as thrilling as driving a car. Za-roosh! Hands on the wheel, foot on the gas, eyes on the road, knees a fist-width apart, elbows just so, shoulders level, ears on high alert, teeth polished to a blinding shine, toenails primly clipped, fingernails the same, shades (outfitted, if required per the optical portion of your "licence to drive," with prescription lenses) perched on your face like a cool buzzard on a tombstone . . . Check? Let's go!

First stop: a winding seaside motorway, with your exhaust pipe belching great plumes of fun. Except with the pedal to the metal actually nothing can stop you—not the pigs, certainly, as you blow by a cruiser secreted behind a Don't Speed sign. They just shake their heads. "Nothing we can do about that," think the two swine impotently, and go back to solving a murder anyway. Today's all about you and your convertible, and everyone knows it. Though what they don't know is that you've named said convertible after a beloved childhood relative—Aunt Brenda, Uncle Turbo, Father, whatever. Maybe it's time to take Father's top down? Yes, there's the good stuff. Everything's unleashed.

Now you can really live. The windscreen catches every bug in sight, saving you an unsolicited snack. And when the glass becomes clotted with their pulverized remains, no matter: a quick flick of the wipers and a squirt of a specially appointed soap smears everything clean. God, what an afternoon, with the ocean pounding the rocks below, "rock" pounding your stereo, the wind in your hair and your heart on fire with automotive lust. "Is this it?" you wonder. Yes, of course it is. This is it.

To drive is to love, to dream and to fly. Even an airplane doesn't provide the same sensation of flying, at least in a metaphorical sense, best exemplified when driving at breakneck speeds through a forest of old-growth timber. Besides, if you tried to take a plane in there you'd destroy every tree within a hundred miles. And not only are you a lover of cars, you're a lover of the woods as well, and all the creatures in it. Even the screeching, godforsaken owls.

Sure, a forest, why not? Cliff-tops aren't the only place for a drive. Even a modest errand might be an occasion for glory. When you pull up to the laundrette and exit your vehicle with a tricky defenestration, it amounts to wearing a sign that announces, "Make way, champion coming through." You'd think a driver removed from their car would be like a dog without a mouth, but it's not like that at all. No, you carry your car in your soul, everywhere you go—compacted into a cube of metal and crammed between lungfuls of your sweetest memories and the spleen of your most ruinous sadness.

What does a driver wear? There's no official uniform, though a scarf, goggles, racing cap and gloves aren't untoward. Nor is a leather trouser that gapes provocatively at the buttocks. Spurs aren't necessary, but they can't hurt either—until you impale a finger. Though of course that's what the gloves are for. For shoes it's best to go with something stylish but athletic, like a loafer. Just hold the pennies. You don't need the extra weight dragging you down. If you own sandals, burn them now.

Driving is one thing, but what about when you have to "pause for because," whether it's for gas, a good lubing or nature's calls? Parking's no problem for you, whether in a lot, garage or paralleled upon the street. Some people struggle with leveraging each of the wheels simultaneously, but for a chauffeur of your calibre it's as easy as one, two, three . . . four. For that's how many wheels there are, and you're a master of them all.

Your colloquial "wheels," too, is (are?) decked out with all the finest accoutrements: bucket seats, trim, fins, hundreds of gears, dozens of mirrors, the perfect number of miles per gallon, and all the dials anyone could ever dream of. Is your car too hot, cold, oily, moist or slow? What time is it, anyway? And which way's north-east? Don't worry, there's a dial for everything, spinning wildly and saving you hours of fruitless guesswork.

What's under the hood? An engine. Feel free to take a look; just "pop the lid" and see. Careful, though—don't touch anything. A single piston can chew through a pound of human flesh lickety-split, leathers be damned. The horsepower is infinite. The valves are pumping, or will be. There's a combustor also, and a carburetor. And what about that thing? Is that where you put the battery? It's all a mystery, never to be solved. To think such a miracle was concocted by human beings, not by gods! In a factory.

All systems go? Time to hit the road. Nothing can keep a motorist of your calibre standing around like an idiot. Flush the toilet, scrub your hands, use a paper towel to turn the soiled knob— then back in the car, where the engine starts with the roar of a million stallions neighing for the attentions of a single rampaging mare. Shades on, brake disengaged, blind spots confirmed, and off you "peel" . . . with a demon's reckless abandon . . . into the pale shreds of the last dying sunset . . . of your freedom . . . *FOREVER*.

THE FOLLOWING WEEK PASSED like clouds across the sky, or sands through an indifferent hourglass with a hole in the bottom. Mr. Ponytail's adoring public flooded the mall in droves, ignoring me resolutely, while I shuffled to and from the food court and tinkered at a provisional Progress Report at my desk. I did not explore the mall. I did not spare a thought for insurrection. I simply bade my time until an opportunity presented itself to venture again to the elevator and descend undetected into the spooky subterranean depths. The truth, I felt, was down there.

The Progress Report I wrote, and summarily abandoned, was a generic piece tangential to my residency. Though it would not be the week's official submission (I feared it might implicate me in some way, as the topic, larceny, ultimately felt "a little too close to my home"), I will include it below for posterity:

Shoplifting is the name for clandestine theft from the mall. Instead of paying for a purchase, there is a special breed of deviant who, through ignorance, indecency, arrogance or pathology, will "lift" said item from a "shop" and abscond. May everyone's gods have mercy on their souls.

Often luggage is involved, or an egregiously baggy trouser. The villain will glance about, left and right, sneak some desired and unearned object into concealment, and then, cool as a spring breeze, waltz out the door to freedom—until they are tackled by security personnel and prosecuted under the full extent of the law. Though there is no law adequately severe for those who defile the mall with thievery. It's like urinating on a church, or in a public toilet roaring "Well, hello there, Grandma!" mid-movement.

Shoplifting is an act of treason. What has the mall ever done to you? Welcomed you with open arms, i.e., doors. Showered you with pleasure. At worst confetti. Perhaps it offered you shelter, or a place to love, or a place to dream—all at affordable rates. But in the face of shoplifting, what option does the goods-depleted proprietor have but to boost their prices? It's simple economics, just as the markets ebb and flow with the cycles of the moon, or one's pay grade varies with a taste for bootlicking the boss.

Who shoplifts? The heartless and degenerate. Losers too. Simply put, if you can't afford a thing you like, then that thing's not for you. It's for someone else with deeper pockets, and you and your miserly shallow pockets ought to traipse on home for another supper of sorrow. You can't simply filch a new pair of pockets, e.g., those garnishing a pair of chic jeans. No: pockets, like jeans, must be earned. So why not apply for a job at the mall? Perhaps the security detail is hiring—with your insider take on the wily machinations of the petty criminal, who better to "serve and/or protect" the mall than you?

Now you're in the thick of it. Baton in hand, crouching behind a rack of dresses like a jaguar among the reeds, lying in wait for the aspiring shoplifter to make a move. "Just try me," you think, having pledged to uphold the honour of the mall with your body, mind and soul. It's true, you'll do anything to protect whatever shop requires your services—a denim concern, certainly, but even a hairdresser. Shoplifters can be so brazen and, frankly, sick that they'll even snatch an unattended comb or scissors.

And if they do? You'll bash their skulls in.

If it comes to that, of course. One prefers a capture. You yourself are the proof of rehabilitation. So when you apprehend a shoplifter—a goofy, drooling fellow with a knick-knack tucked up his sleeve—you do so almost tenderly. You take him out at the knees, sure, but the way you get him to the ground is like an angel laying a sinner to rest. And there, with your baton pressed to his throat, you tell him that the proof's in the pudding.

But why go rooting around inside a delicious dessert for evidence? All you need to do is strip the guy nude and there it is: a sunflower tchotchke, the sort anyone would love to get their hands on. Yet more decent souls would never dare shoplift an item of such quality and worth. Ten dollars, $19.99, 401(k)—whatever the price—we'd pay it, such is our reverence for the mall, the shops and the goods therein.

"Why yes," one thinks, "I think at last I'll purchase this swell item for which I've 'pinched pennies' for years, the whole while battling with the knave in me who'd just as soon swipe it from the shelf . . . And so, having thwarted those fiendish impulses, here I am and here's my money, and no, that's fine, no need for a bag, I'm wearing it home, proud as a peacock with its regalia fanned in full glory, for I want everyone who sees me to witness the delicious, honourable fruits of transacting money for goods instead of the treachery of shoplifting, which debases us all . . . But now, Sir and/or Madam Proprietor, let's both return to our respective lives with the jubilant song of commerce in our hearts, for today everyone's a winner, aren't they, from you the vendor and me the customer to anyone else in the world who recognizes that the only worthy 'shoplifting' is this: the uplift of one's spirits aroused by shopping."

By the end of the week I'd recognized this little essay as a work of recklessness and was feeling a bit despondent as I headed for lunch: What else might I write about? What progress was I making—or might I pretend to be?

I arrived at the food court to discover it teeming with even more Ponytail acolytes than before. The seating area was so crowded that some people ate standing, like barbarians. The air reeked of grease and sweat and sycophancy. Despite having shaved it dutifully that morning, I felt my tongue-hair twitch.

With my jaw locked grimly, I joined a massive line snaking from the chicken stand all the way to the escalators, and spent the next forty-five minutes plodding forward incrementally, suffering a chorus of enthusiasms about my nemesis and all that he had done, all that he was and all that he might yet become.

Finally I reached the counter and placed my order, yet was dispatched to a waiting area for another twenty minutes. By the time I collected my tray, rage had filled my belly so amply that I was no longer hungry, and I wheeled to face the food court with every intention of making a great show, for all to see, of stalking straight to the garbage area and dumping my lunch "straight down the hatch."

But the mob was dispersing. Everyone was heading upstairs en masse, while a harried K. Sohail was trying her best, solo, to direct foot traffic, maintain decorum, ensure the escalator wasn't overloaded, and hastily snack through a "two-piece" prepared for her by the chicken teens. Most shockingly, the chicken teens themselves were packing up and joining the throng. The mall's pre-eminent resident was up to something, clearly, and everyone was rushing to catch his inane matinee.

Everyone except me, of course.

How delicious that my rival provided the distraction I'd been waiting for! With the mall's first floor as vacant as the dull, glazed expressions of Mr. Ponytail's opiated devotees, I slipped off to the service elevator, climbed inside and punched the anonymous lozenge. It glowed like a moon, and the erratic contraption juddered into motion. Here goes nothingness, I thought: where would I be taken this time?

Again the elevator dropped, and zigged and zagged, and, after a few minutes, finally landed, though this time with less a bracing shudder than almost gently, as if eased to rest by an unseen hand (or horde of ponytails). I cracked the doors and peered out: no sign of any hair; the view was dim, but at least the coast seemed clear.

I'd ended up at neither the swimming pool nor the parking garage, but the corridor of an industrial area that curled out of view. The lighting here was sparse and yellow, from somewhere distant came the roar of a furnace, and a sulphuric odour haunted the air. I was in the bowels of the mall now, for sure. Which made me wonder: were I to continue downward, might I eventually find freedom via its anus?

The truth about the mall was not going to be pretty.

I stepped out of the elevator and stood there for a moment, taking in "the view." A low ceiling was veined with exposed, dripping pipes and wires pulsing with current, and every twenty feet or so lamps cast splotches of coppery light on the damp cement floor. This felt less like the hallways of the mall than a tunnel spiralling inward to some central hub. The whole place, dim and dank, sent dread shuddering through my soul: something terrible was down here, I was sure of it.

But then I pictured Dennis, and Klassanderella. I had hero's work to do. I kissed my ring and pushed ahead. For now, my tongue-hair lay dormant and subdued.

A morbid symphony accompanied my infiltration: the rhythmic tinkle of the pipes, the distant breath of the furnace, the hum of the wires, the tap of my footsteps. Between lamplit stations I could see nothing in the shadows, and the tunnel curled interminably, whatever was around the corner always just out of view. I moved on instinct alone.

And this realization gave me pause. Wasn't instinctual behaviour precisely what the mall wanted? For me to be seduced by what felt like intuition and to believe that said intuition was my own, when in fact the mall had infiltrated my thoughts? Six weeks here had no doubt reprogrammed my brain to the mall's diabolical caprices. The result of which, I feared, was to end up like Dennis, drowned and partially scalped. And I didn't even have a ponytail! God knows what part of me would mutiny against my own body.

Walking along, I regarded my legs skeptically. Is that what they'd been up to in the parking garage? Had they willingly trapped themselves with the hope of being severed from my torso so they could head off on their own, either joining Mr. Ponytail's army or mounting their own leggy insurrection? I pictured them autonomously goose-stepping about the mall. And me dragging myself behind on a pair of stumps.

I shivered. I needed to keep a handle on all my parts—legs, arms, ears, nether regions, whatever. Apparently "everything must go," or could, in the great clearinghouse extravaganza of the mall's "final sale." Poor Dennis, I thought again, following the curling tunnel toward its elusive centre, longing for a weapon— even the chicken skewer I'd abandoned in the parking garage. How I'd brandish it now like a sabre, prepared to flay without mercy whatever enemy might be lurking in the dark!

Weapon or none, stalking the mall's "corridors of power" was real work. What a revelatory Progress Report I could write about these excursions. The toil and struggle. The *progress*. And dare I say the *engagement* too? Admittedly there wasn't much of a public down here. Even so, I hadn't felt so engaged in weeks. And wasn't this the mark of a true worker? Self-engagement? For what is work without fulfillment of the self? Yes, I thought: the world works best when everyone in the world is working, and work makes the world go round.

Though was that right? Sure, it was a dandy of an aphorism, but did it capture some essential "colonel of truth"? I was struggling to form clear thoughts as I waded through the mind-muddling darkness, the tunnel curving inward but never reaching its terminus. What if it merely circled back to the elevator?

God, the mall was sick. Yet I continued on, with the bend of the wall endlessly obscuring what might lie around the corner— so far, just more wall. I began to feel that I was teetering toward an abyss. Every twenty yards I'd step into a pale splash of light, like a bucket of yellow paint tipped down from the ceiling. Ceiling? Such a thing wasn't even visible beyond that snaking network of pipes and wires, humming and ticking, emitting the occasional hiss of steam.

Was it a ceiling *of* pipes and wires? Was that possible? Could mere pipes and wires uphold the weight of the floor above?

I stopped short: a ceiling was just another floor's floor! Wasn't it?

I tried to gather my thoughts as I continued—but they swirled like frantic searchlights through the gloom of my mind.

If this ceiling, pipes and wires or not, was the floor of the floor above—say, the parking garage, that orgy of demented cars and ponytails—what then comprised the respective ceiling of the floor I now walked upon? If this industrial area, itself a basement, had a sub-basement, how did one account, ceiling-wise, for *its* floor? How far down could the whole floor/ceiling arrangement go? Sub-sub? Sub-sub-sub? Sub-sub-sub-sub, all the way until it met the curve of the earth and circled back to reconnect with the mall's second storey, where a ceiling-cum-floor became a kind of roof?

And what then? When did a sub cease to be a sub? To become, say, super?

My confusion extended to other subs—*sub*marines, *sub*traction, *sub*terfuge, *sub*contractor. Were there multiple levels of those too? Where did it end?

And what was a subcontractor anyway? *Sub*: under; *con*: against; but what about *tractor*? If traction meant pulling, or something like it, then *tractor*, generally, had to signify the functional apparatus, mechanized and farmer-piloted or otherwise.

So then a *sub-con-tractor* must undermine the very act of pulling. But such as what?

Such as maybe a wall? Which by its sheer, blithe inertness was certainly anti-pull.

Or would a subcontractor, in order to earn its *con*, have to actively, if *subtly*, push? For example, I thought, a door with the word Push on it—a sly suggestion, offering the pedestrian no option. Imagine you are being chased. What else to do but follow the instructions and become a subcontractor in the process. Was I a subcontractor, then, having pushed my way through a lifetime of doors, figurative and literal?

How then did that explain a *subcontract*? *Contract*, of course, meaning "to shrink." How did one get under that? Perhaps I needed once again to break the word down into its component parts. So to be under (*sub*) and against (*con*) some alleged *tract*—as in a manifesto? or a parcel of land? Assuming the former, I imagined infiltrating a meeting of revolutionaries as an agent of the state, operating undercover (subcover?), attending their meetings and nodding agreeably through every speech and missive, albeit while covertly undermining (submining?) the actual manifesto-writing process with defeatist suggestions and counterintuitive edits, such that when it was eventually published the document would be unconvincing and rally no one, and the group would disband in shame. Or was it the latter *tract*: poisoning a rival's soil with plague.

*Sub*poena—under *poena*, sure. But what in god's name was a poena? I tried to locate that strange pairing of syllables elsewhere in my vocabulary: *peon* was close but inverted the vowels; *poem* might do at a glance but on closer inspection snuck an extra hump into its lettering and dropped the *a*; *Pina* was both a woman's name and the fruity ingredient of a sweet, slushy drink. Under Pina? Surely not!

I stopped walking. Took my head in my hands and physically shook it free of thoughts—too much! Too much!

Was I losing it?

Worse, I thought. Ahead of me the wall curved into gloom; behind me the same. I was nowhere. I was lost. For a long time I'd been lost.

I gazed up at the entropy of pipes and wires above, twining and twisting off into the darkness—so like neurological pathways. Which made the security lights the synaptic explosions of sense and thought! So a brain, then. This wasn't the mall's guts, but a kind of cranial holding centre, and here I was, lost in it—not just physically, but mentally too.

Considering how wildly my thoughts had been careering around, was it not possible that these strange, meandering tunnels were in fact passageways through *my own brain*? Which made me not just lost in thought but lost in *my* thoughts—and not just lost to myself but lost *in* myself! My neuroses had literally consumed me. And now there was no way back. Back to what? I struggled to remember where I'd come from, where I was meant to be going . . . It was as if I'd gotten halfway to something definitive and suffered a stroke, rendering me disoriented and adrift.

I looked around: everything was uniformly dim, the hallway curling identically in both directions and the pipes and wires snaking along above, still with no suggestion that one direction led anywhere more conclusive than its opposite. Were I to turn around and head back, would I be returning home or simply continuing on this same exploratory path? Could it be a loop? An interminable spiral? Or the inwardly vacuuming coils of a black hole that would swallow me into madness?

Perhaps I could think my way out.

No: thinking was precisely what had gotten me into this mess.

The key, I thought, was to *unthink*.

Let this be my last thought, I thought. And with that I sat on the concrete floor—its damp touch greeting my buttocks—closed my eyes and did my best to erase consciousness from my brain. To wash my cortex clean, as it were; to gain clarity. I concentrated on my breathing, in and out. I rejected any mental image, any external sensation. I let go of language, of memory, of worry and fear and even—Klassanderella!—love. I ceased to fear the void. I welcomed it. When some perception or idea or quandary came swimming up, I pushed it under (*sub*). A faint scent of sulphur—suppressed. A leg cramp—ignored. Sudden concern about the plight of an elegant bird species I'd not seen since childhood—not really relevant.

But after five minutes or so of this I became a little too aware of the single piece of stubble growing from my tongue—which, upon any break in the action, became so acutely felt as to drive me bonkers—and rocketed to my feet. Fighting my own mind into stillness was absurd; the abyss would always dwell beyond the scrim of consciousness that separated me and true oblivion. And I wasn't about to kill myself to get there.

What an idiotic exercise, I thought, and continued on my way.

Who cares to see oneself clearly? To reduce one's thoughts to a blank slate, and one's self-perception to something essential and intrinsic, wherein one—or, more specifically, *I*—emerged pure and unburdened of all the psychological baggage that had obfuscated my sense of self. How the hell would *that* get me home? And even if it did, then I'd have to deal with whatever terrifying realizations my subconscious had unearthed. No, indeed. Those sorts of insights were best buried in the basement—

And then it struck me: *the basement.* The mall! It all came back—or at least some of it. I mean, who was to say if what I remembered in that instant was, in fact, everything. Chances are, probably not. Memory being, of course, not only subjective but the moth-eaten net through which not just negligible bycatch but perhaps even momentous fish escape. What is remembering but dredging up the residue of experience—the weakest sea life that couldn't fight its way to freedom. And *this* informs who we are?

No, I thought. I'd rather exist as lack, as a sort of negative space—an apparition, a cypher. What made me myself should remain mysterious. Not a fabrication of contrived recollections. That's not what made me. *I* was all the stuff swimming loose in the ether of the unremembered, the unconsidered, the unknowable and unknown—what drifted out there beyond me. So what to do but keep walking, I thought—into the darkness, with my mind and body like a sieve through which life might pass: nothing catching, nothing holding. I would proceed as an ephemeral wisp through existence, never any closer to becoming whoever I might actually be.

On further reflection, this didn't make much sense either. And this endless walking was getting boring. But which way to go? Back or forward? Either the dank and frankly depressing corridor spiralled interminably toward an ever-elusive centre or it curled back in a circle to the elevator. Considering the size of the mall, I could still be miles from the terminus, while turning back would double my travel time. And there was no way I could take twice as much walking as I'd already done.

Despite the claims of a certain abandoned Progress Report, I've never had much patience with ambulation as a leisure activity. One ought to go *places*, I'd long thought, not simply *go*; and besides, we'd invented bicycles to save us from the stultifying labour of footwork. Already the past—what? hour? ninety minutes? day?—had been insufferable and pointless. And now, underdressed in nothing but shirtsleeves and stylishly torn albeit drafty jeans, I was also fed up with the damp chill down here, not to mention that, having forgone my midday meal, I was incredibly hungry as well.

This level of the mall, it seemed, was designed only to test my patience. And it was working. My spirits were flagging. What a fool I'd been to discard my skewer-sword and armour! If a foe were to leap now from the shadows they'd do me in lickety-split. And then I'd be nothing but a waste of good denim.

And here again the ghost of Dennis urged me on. Not literally, of course. If only some sort of post-Dennis spectre would come sifting out of the shadows and with a clank of his chains deliver some cryptic yet informative set of directions to lead me to freedom. No, there were no ghosts down here.

But there was a horse.

I heard the clop of its hooves before I saw it coming round the bend. And then we were face to face, maybe a yard or two apart. Obscured in shadow, the animal paused. Snorted gently. Tossed its mane. The coat was a light colour, beige or grey. The smells were rustic. The head drooped with sedate deference. A small horse. Having some experience with equestrian measurements, I guessed its height at fifteen hands. Or fewer? I examined my palm and did a quick calculation, mentally severing my hand from my arm and stacking it fingertips-to-heel up the flank . . .

Twelve. The horse stood a dozen hands tall. Which meant, per equine specifications, this was no horse!

The creature before me was in fact a pony.

FOR MANY, THE SUDDEN ARRIVAL of a midsize animal (equine, bovine, venison) in the subterranean recesses of a shopping centre might be a source of alarm, even upset. But, as I've mentioned, having spent some time in equestrian circles—or at least "at the track"—I find horses quite soothing. Their gaze, their bearing, their sleek and placid way. Horses express to me a great equanimity and peacefulness. Ponies especially. Certainly their size helps. (A great Clydesdale trundling out of the shadows might have had a different effect.) But, at any rate, the pony set me at ease.

I made my approach at a slight angle, whispering soothing and complimentary words (*Aren't you a comely creature*, etc.), a hand extended in a gesture of supplication. He gave my fingers a sniff and seemed unperturbed, so I settled them on his neck for a gentle massage, checking the undercarriage to confirm his gender: male, indeed! Even in the dim light of the industrial sector I could see wisdom and serenity in his eyes. And yet something haunting and haunted, too . . .

I stepped back. There was a lack to this pony, I thought. A lack, perhaps, that mirrored one I'd long sensed in myself—and which, certainly, had been accentuated since the beginning of this residency, preying as it did on my every insecurity. (A lack turned explicit when my only friend was murdered and my beloved was thousands of miles to the southeast tending to her dying mother. Never mind the profound inadequacies Mr. Ponytail inspired!)

A glance at the pony's hindquarters confirmed it:

The fellow had no tail!

But I had no time to compare inadequacies. He'd come here to show me something, to take me somewhere, and with a nod and a snort he was quickly on the move. Clearly I was meant to follow him. I recalled some old maxim about being led by a horse to water . . . Yet surely I wasn't obliged to drink anything. And what did I have to lose? The pony had come from somewhere. For hours I'd been circling this stupid basement with no end in sight. I was nowhere. And anywhere was better than that.

So I "took to my heels" and followed that mysterious, tailless pony as he tramped off into the darkness, the initial shock of his unfestooned buttocks now, as I fixed my eyes upon them, ceding to sadness. They were so tragically reminiscent of my whole reason for being (at least down here, in the mall's underground industrial sector): Dennis, that is. My former best friend and current martyr. For whom vengeance would soon be mine— I just had to dare utter the phrase aloud first.

Before we could proceed, the pony would need a name. Never a task to take lightly. Naming an animal is a delicate affair. Especially an animal that one might enjoy for companionship rather than meat. You peer into their eyes, put your hand on their heart (if they'll let you) and listen as their name speaks itself from within—from within the animal, that is, but within yourself as well, as if the souls of man or woman and beast are communing. *This is who I am*, whispers the creature's soul to your soul. And then you say their name aloud, and then they come.

Have I ever given an animal the wrong name? Yes. Instead of listening (viz. the process described above), I *gave* it to her—a cat, Sharon (or so I thought), who, after fourteen painstaking years of a clear identity crisis that involved her spending entire days staring out the window into the rain or chewing the beaks off small birds, as well as thoroughly ignoring me at every turn (she never came once when I called), on her deathbed finally revealed to me the truth: her name was in fact *Karen*. And then she was gone.

Burying that poor, misnomered cat in the yard, I told myself that I'd never make the same mistake again. I'd not speak; I'd listen. That said, I was willing to swear on Sharon/Karen's grave that my new equine friend was . . . Gary. And I believed this so heartily because I didn't name him at all. I didn't have to. He just *was* Gary.

He was Gary in the measured, dutiful and pensive way that he plodded along the industrial corridor; Gary in the methodical and rhythmic bob of his head; Gary in the sombre yet considerate gaze that he occasionally flung over his shoulder to make sure I was keeping up; Gary in his unbridled (no pun) acceptance of me as a kind of interspecific sibling; Gary in the trust he elicited as I followed obediently behind. (So I was the one "coming," in a way. And I came and came and came, everywhere that Gary went.)

Where did Gary go? For a while I felt we were just navigating the same circuit that I'd been walking so hopelessly on my own. But Gary had a few tricks up his proverbial sleeve, or should I say mane. In one of those intermittent swaths of darkness between the security lights, he paused. Waiting for him to continue, I was acutely aware of his lack of tail: nothing swished through the shadows; nothing dangled between his legs beyond the more utilitarian anatomy. A pony with no tail is a curious sight, like a house with no windows: not essential, though they do make for a nicer view. I wondered if he'd had an accident or been attacked; was what I'd taken for melancholy actually the restrained anguish of a survivor?

But there was no time for further speculation because—was it? yes!—from within the shadows an elevator was opening. Not *the* elevator: this was larger, a little more sterile. The sort one finds in a hospital. Roomy enough for a coffin, or even two or three in a pinch. As with the other elevator there was only one button, I discovered, as I squeezed in beside Gary and the door closed behind me. He neighed softly; the indication was clear. I pressed the button. And the thing sprung to life, and Gary nodded, and down—or up?—we went.

For anyone who's ridden an elevator with a pony, tailed or no, what follows might be redundant. But for those who haven't, it's needless to say that even the most sedate animals can become unsettled by disembodied movement through space. Gary was a serene creature indeed, and admirable for his restraint, but I could sense that as we plummeted (or rose? or travelled on a horizontal axis?) through miles of subterranean mall that he was growing increasingly antsy. For a pony wants to prance, not stand idly by while a mechanical contraption hauls them up and/or down and/or across some shaft.

So I took the liberty of laying a placating hand on Gary's silver flank and bidding him, Shh. There, I cooed, who's a clever pony?

The question was rhetorical (obvious answer: Gary), but it elicited the intended response. I felt his muscles relax. Surely he'd ridden this elevator before, so maybe all I offered was camaraderie and understanding. Though I wondered too if his tension wasn't merely anticipatory. Maybe the elevator doors would open on a vast and archetypal meadow, butterflies flitting about a riot of lilacs, with a whole herd of ponies romping around. Gary's brothers and sisters—finally he was home!

How I longed to see him run, all that glory unleashed. Or to munch some hay.

But why would he have fetched me then? Simply to show off? No, I expected that Gary had some greater purpose in mind. I felt anointed, chosen—and also, to be fair, rescued. With my hand on his haunches, the two of us zipping through space toward destinations unknown (to me, that is; Gary probably knew), I thought about my purposes—to solve and redeem the diabolical mystery of Dennis's murder, to uncover the fraudulence of Mr. Ponytail, to flee to Klassanderella and marry her expertly. And now I had an ally. And perhaps, wherever we were headed, there were more of us still.

It was here that I began to "piece together the puzzle," though with the following discoveries came the larger, more humiliating realization that this alleged puzzle was in fact a fully formed picture that had been staring me in the face the entire time. My deductions were akin to pointing at an exquisitely rendered painting of a horse and screaming *Horse!* at the top of one's lungs.

The key was this: no pony . . . tail. No ponytail!

Of course Gary and I were "playing for the same team." He'd been down in the industrial sector for the same reasons I had: the pursuit of justice. Like Dennis he'd been de-tailed—viciously, humiliatingly—though somehow, perhaps because he wasn't human, he'd escaped the same mortal fate. And now we'd found each other and formed a sort of retributive task force. On my own I'd been a lone vigilante, something of a renegade, and possibly weird. But now, equipped with both posse and steed (even if both were embodied in the same animal), I gained legitimacy. And power. And prestige!

Did this mean I should mount Gary? Not yet—probably.

AFTER A TIME—again, impossible to say how long—the elevator slowed and stopped. I sensed we'd travelled in circles, though that might just have been a holdover from endlessly coiling around the industrial sector, going insane. The doors opened. What appeared wasn't a meadow of frolicking ponies. Before us, in a shimmering rectangle the colour of tears, sat the mall's one and only swimming pool.

My first thought, of course, was of Dennis. But no body floated in the water. Which meant that someone had come and scooped his carcass from the pool, and perhaps even performed some sort of last rites (or else discarded him with the trash). K. Sohail seemed a likely suspect either way—out of her own innate decency, or per the callous protocols of the mall. For now, though, no one was here. The water trembled slightly, its reflection shimmering up the walls. Everything seemed so clean, so sterile. That a murder had ever happened here seemed not just improbable but absurd.

Gary nudged me gently with his nose. I was to step "on deck." But what if this was a trick or a trap? I gazed into the pony's eyes. No, this animal was looking out for me: what I saw there was truth, honesty, understanding. Possibly even love. I would not be duped by Gary. He'd definitely brought me here to show me something.

I went up to the edge of the pool and peered into the water. Nothing. Not even my own reflection. The surface swelled and ebbed like an epidermis rising and falling with each living breath. I looked back to Gary for help, or advice. But he only neighed softly, seeming to urge me forward. My god—was I meant to *swim*?

I believe I have mentioned elsewhere my incapacity for watersport. Simply put, I sink. However, Gary had brought me here—perhaps at risk to his own safety. And I felt I would be letting him down if I didn't at least wade into the pool and have a poke around. So I boldly disrobed down to my undergarments, toed the water—warm enough—and eased in, while Gary watched from the elevator.

Clutching the side of the pool I surveyed things at eye level. Nothing of note. Gary snorted. I interpreted this to mean *go under*. So I dunked my head, eyes open, and peered into the pool.

The water was full of ghosts.

No: the water *was* ghosts.

They swarmed about wispily, a great traffic of them, twining past and between and through one another, like the cellular components of human blood. Though their forms weren't human. None had a face. They weren't bodies, but actual spirits: souls, I thought. Was Dennis's among them? I searched the throng for his eager way—a single jolly character darting about with guileless abandon—but couldn't distinguish one ghost from the rest. Also I was running out of air.

I surfaced for breath, gasping. Outside the water, the phantoms below were invisible. So I inhaled a lungful of air, plunged face-first again, and they reappeared, busily swirling around. Maybe a thousand ghosts, maybe more. And they seemed either not to notice me or not to care, plunging this way and that—with the express purpose, it seemed, of *being water*. Such that their movement seemed to create a kind of energy. A hydrologic energy, I thought, that might be used to power something. That could, in fact, power an entire shopping mall.

I surfaced. So, I asked Gary, was this the big secret? That the mall sacrificed its proprietors, severed their ponytails and enslaved their spirits to cut back on electric bills? Gary only stared. I went under again to watch the ghosts, to try to glean some understanding of their plight. How might I set them free? Drain the pool? Flood it?

But, watching them with this new-found intention, I didn't sense misery. There was a certain dignity to the dutiful way they swam about. Who was I to decide they needed liberating? Though of course the caged bird doesn't necessarily appreciate the thrill of flight until she is unleashed skyward . . . Maybe only upon their emancipation would the ghosts realize what they'd been missing—the world and all that was in it!

I came up again for air.

One would think, I thought as I clung to the side of the pool, that a key discovery along the way to solving a crime would inspire action or at least strengthen one's resolve. But the more I learned about the mall, the more powerless I felt—and, perversely enough, the less I grasped.

How could I, a person who resided here free of charge, who produced dubious Progress Reports to validate said arrangement, and who had been usurped by a renegade length of human hair, be expected to understand a poolful of ghosts? Their presence didn't activate my inner vigilante; it only humbled me more.

And further to that: So what if I even figured out who or what had killed Dennis, and how? What could I do with that information? In what court would justice be served?

No, I thought, pushing away from the pool and sitting there dripping on the deck—under the watchful eye of Gary, who'd brought me here with intimations of solidarity and, I sensed, hope that I might be the one to take action. What could I do? I was no saviour. Not of ghosts, not of ponies, not of the down-trodden denizens of the mall.

And possibly not even of myself.

Hold on a minute.

When had I become so maudlin? Before moving into the mall I hadn't exactly been a "go-getter," but at least I'd been capable of going and getting through an average day with my chin held level if not high. I would have once considered myself an enthusiast, the sort of person inspired to act, even if said actions were more often felt—with passion!—rather than actually performed.

For example, whether it was the worst mistake of my life or not, I'd had the confidence to apply for this residency. I used to believe in myself! And now I'd been reduced to a withered, pathetic, snivelling thing, dripping on the deck of a ghost-filled swimming pool while an honourable, helpful pony looked on, bemused.

It was time, for once in my recent life, to *do something*.

So I dropped to my knees, cupped my hands, swept up some water from the pool, and drank it to the last drop.

Yes, indeed: I drank a ghost.

I could feel it slithering down my throat—not cold, not warm, not unpleasant. Just a tepid, slightly gelatinous slurp that settled in my guts in a little puddle.

Rising to my full, glorious height, I puffed out my chest a little. I'd taken action, been resolute, hadn't dithered. An opportunity had presented itself and I'd seized it. And what a canny move I'd made: now I might, with one of their species inside me, better understand what help I might be to the ghosts. My god, I'd never felt so alive!

Gary appeared to feel otherwise.

Having stepped from the elevator onto the deck of the pool—presumably to stop me—he clomped his hoof and shook his head. *No*, he seemed to be saying. *No, no, no.*

I'd made a terrible mistake.

And alongside this horrible sinking feeling came the distinct sensation that I'd swallowed not one ghost, but two. And now they were battling for real estate, in their swirly way, among my internal organs. The feeling was somewhere between the first black inklings of a fast-metastasizing intestinal cancer and gas—a sort of hollow, dizzy swoon that swam around my stomach and southward, precipitously approaching my colon before doubling back.

Gary, I cried. I'm sorry! I shouldn't have drunk two ghosts!

But Gary only eyed the elevator—furtively, as the captain of a doomed spacecraft might its sole escape pod.

I collected my clothes and rushed at him, eyebrows arched in supplication. In apology. But as I ran, my feet lifted from the deck, churning air. I was floating. Maybe six inches off the tiles. Floating! In my stomach the ghosts were writhing over each other like lusty eels. So not only did they make me gassy; they made me float.

Gary shook his head: *Now see what you've done.*

Hovering six inches above the deck, I tried a breaststroke. Made a little progress, though slowly. But with no resistance from the air I couldn't propel myself with much force. And Gary's disappointed gaze weighed me down.

I stopped swimming and sank back to the deck. Cautiously took a step. But it was as if magnets on the soles of my feet were repulsed by a corresponding charge. I couldn't make contact, couldn't walk. Any movement only boosted me airborne.

So, hovering, I put on my jeans—the jeans, now, of abjection. And also my shirt (less disgraceful, but still not triumphant or anything). Then, fully clothed, I stilled my limbs and lowered to the deck again.

Remaining as motionless as possible, I asked Gary what was to be done.

And though I'd failed him, though he'd rescued me from the industrial sector and generously brought me to the "scene of the crime," and though I'd shamed us both by swallowing ghosts and rendering myself even more useless than ever, he made a noise I can only describe as a sigh. He trudged forward, ducked his head and paused at my side.

Mount me, he seemed to be saying.

So I grabbed a handful of mane and hauled myself aboard.

And Gary, like a soldier—or, more so, like a medic rescuing a wounded soldier from a carnage-strewn battlefield—plodded into the elevator to take me somewhere new.

WITH THE RIGIDITY OF THINGS UNSAID, of one who prides himself on maintaining "stiffened lips" in the face of even the most profound disgrace, Gary stood unmoving in the elevator with me atop his back. Gary, I wanted to cry, I've failed you! But his silence was my punishment. Or, rather, his silence confronted me with all that I'd done wrong. To break it would be to forgo his forgiveness forever.

So I accepted my punishment and thought. What had I done wrong? I'd swallowed ghosts. I'd breached protocol and compromised Gary. Gary, my saviour, who only wanted the best for me, who clearly had suffered from or at least was at odds with Mr. Ponytail and his legions, and possibly the mall as well. We'd been a team. And what were we now? Literally he carried me. I'd become a burden.

Still, what a towering figure of integrity he was, to hold me aloft, to even lead me further on my quest for justice (if that's where we were headed; perhaps he was taking me to a cell or sacrificial lair—who was to say?) At any rate, Gary had a job to do and by god he was doing it. Was this job, though, the same as mine? He'd taken me to the site of Dennis's murder, or at least disposal, but how I was meant to use this information to help us both was still a mystery.

As the elevator continued its voyage through space and, it seemed, time (though isn't one always travelling through time, even when motionless, such as it is to be alive?), a new feeling darkened the edges of my shame. Not resentment, exactly. More irritation. Sure, I definitely shouldn't have drunk from the ghostly waters to which the horse/pony had led me (fool! if only I'd heeded the cliché), but with no clear instructions, how was I expected to behave?

And it wasn't as if I'd scooped the ghosts from the pool and forced them down Gary's throat. I was the one with the things swimming around my guts.

No, if anything it was I who should be perturbed—not Gary. There was something a little smug about his forbearance. And I wondered, also, if he hadn't in some way recruited me selfishly. Perhaps retrieving his tail would present tasks that escaped a pony's capabilities. Forms to fill out, a tree to climb. Or even a single, simple sentence spoken aloud in human language.

That was it: Gary needed me more than I needed him.

And so, rather than begging his forgiveness, I decided to *forgive him*. Mentally, of course. The pony outweighed me by three hundred pounds. I wasn't about to start a fight in the confines of the elevator; I'd be trampled to death in seconds. But at least now we were back on equal footing. I'm not sure if Gary could intuit this—horses/ponies having excellent powers of perception—but I did sense a redistribution of his weight, as if something had shifted within him. Yes! I was the human, the master—the boss. I would not be judged. I would ride Gary however I liked.

The elevator slowed. Stopped. The lit button extinguished. Gary seemed to prepare himself for something monumental. And the ghosts readied themselves as well, tensing . . .

The doors opened.

A hallway led from the elevator to a cage at the far end, in which a woman sat behind a pane of glass that separated—or protected—her from us. Behind her were shelves and cubbies that overflowed with shoes, hats, electronics, various unidentifiable bric-a-brac—and, I noticed, jeans. There was a section of storage dedicated to denim in tidy blue stacks. The woman at the desk nodded cordially. An invitation. But to what?

Where are we? I whispered to Gary. What is this place?

He nodded toward a sign above the woman's head: LOST &/ OR FOUND.

The woman running this operation wore the same beige outfit and peaked cap as K. Sohail, though her nametag claimed her as a certain D. Lee. And unlike K. Sohail, D. Lee seemed grateful to see us. She smiled and straightened and fairly welcomed us with the open arms of a possible embrace, prevented only by the pane of glass.

I drove Gary forward with careful, slow steps so as not to provoke the ghosts into making me float. Upon reaching the cage, I leaned down and spoke to D. Lee through a disc of perforations in the glass.

Hello, I said.

She beamed and asked how we were, how she could help us,

if we were looking for something in particular; the Lost &/or Found had it all.

I told her I wasn't sure. I told her that Gary had brought me here, indicating the pony, and that I was on a quest for truth. I didn't mention Dennis or his murder; D. Lee was, after all, an employee of the mall and her geniality could well be a ruse to lull me (and Gary) into revealing our true purpose (retribution). I told her instead that I was interested in her selection of denim, stepping back slightly so that D. Lee might appreciate my own sartorial sophistication, at least from the waist down, and might I have a look at a pair or two in my size?

D. Lee informed me—not condescendingly, just firmly— that this wasn't a store. The Lost &/or Found contained goods either lost, found or both, and while she might help locate something I'd lost or relieve me of something I'd found and with god's will return it to its rightful owner, she wasn't about to start hauling jeans off her shelves for casual perusal, even if I was an aficionado.

Return it to its rightful owner . . .

Instinctively I hid my hand—but then felt the call of destiny. I removed the ring. Placed it on a tray beneath the speaker. And asked, with a quiver of guilt in my voice, where it might have come from.

The tray swivelled around. On the other side of the glass, D. Lee examined the ring. Held it up to the light. Read the inscription—and gasped. *Now you are mine*, she whispered. Stillness settled over the small room. Even the ghosts quit jostling around my guts. In anticipation, I assumed, or deference—or terror.

D. Lee shook her head sharply, as if to dislodge a thought, placed the ring back in the tray and returned it to me. I can't help you, she said, her voice trembling.

The ring stared up at me like an unblinking, judgmental eye. Retrieving it would be to accept D. Lee's obvious lie, to make myself complicit and to bow to the mall's power. But Gary was watching. I would not forsake him again. (Though, of course, I took the ring—it looked too good on my hand to concede it to the Lost &/or Found, especially as nothing more than a symbol.)

Boldly I told D. Lee the ring's story of origin: the food court, the couple, the retching, the projectile arc, the outfitting, and the ensuing guilt that I bore wearing it on my finger. I didn't mention how said guilt had mostly subsided thanks to the ring's splendid fit, but I wondered if that weren't obvious by how I brandished it with a certain pride.

Avoiding my gaze—the harsh glare of truth—D. Lee turned to the shelves, straightened a clock radio and claimed again that she couldn't help.

I don't accept that, I said, pleased with my perseverance; even the ghosts seemed to swell with a kind of parasitical vanity. But what had I been asking? My thoughts swirled. I checked my hand—right! The ring. I held it up, *demanding* to know where it came from, what the inscription meant, who was addressed by "you" and "mine," and, should D. Lee accept the ring as lost property, to whom it would be returned—Dennis's killer, I privately speculated (but didn't say because of a lack of proof, causality or logic).

Her back still to me, D. Lee again said only: I can't help you. It's not worth it, she said.

Adding: There are forces at work here that you can't possibly understand.

I explained that my understanding was irrelevant; I was not particularly gifted with the powers of rational thought, comprehension and action, so what did it matter? I told D. Lee that I was well aware that something spooky and weird was afoot in the mall—and here I felt that a disclosure might help engender trust, so I said simply, Look, and stuck out my tongue, revealing the unshorn hair, now some two inches long.

D. Lee glanced over her shoulder. Sighed, nodded. Came up to the glass. And, to my shock, stuck out her own tongue.

By god, she had one too!

Flaxen and wispy, slightly curled, the hair trailed from the end of D. Lee's tongue like a rope flung over the edge of a cliff. Twice as long as my own. For a moment we stood like that, tongues out on either side of the glass, hairs on full display. I have rarely felt so connected to another human being—in misery, in persecution, in shame. And the hairs, for their part, began to rouse themselves, wobbling upright like plants to the light . . .

D. Lee closed her mouth first.

For a while I trimmed it, she said, but it grows so fast I gave up.

I asked if it had ceased growing—or would the thing unfurl forever, eventually strangling her or forming some make of single-strand beard?

D. Lee smiled sadly. No, no, she said. It stops after a while.

We exchanged a long and knowing look. Broken only when, with a sigh, she spun the tray around again, picked up the ring and held it to the glass.

Do you really want to know about this? she asked.

I told her yes.

Okay, said D. Lee, told me to hold on, and shuffled off into the back alleys of the Lost &/or Found.

To fetch what? I wondered. Or whom? Klassanderella? Perhaps my beloved had travelled from the islands to find me, gotten bewildered in the mall, boarded the elevator and pushed the wrong button, ended up in the basement, and stashed herself amid the forgone stock with distant hopes of rescue (by me)? Was she lost?

Or perhaps this was a delightful ceremonial game played in Klassanderella's homeland, a premarital turn of "hidden and sought" wherein one's lover secrets him- or herself in a Lost &/or Found, only to be "returned" upon the other's arrival therein?

My heart juddered with anticipation. Surely that was it. I'd nearly forgotten that Klassanderella had a ring just like mine! This seemingly pointless voyage down through the various basements of the mall would culminate now, at last, with a reunion. Yes, I was living a love story that had at last reached its giddily happy ending. I pressed my face to the glass and peered into that dim warren of shelves. I wanted to see Klassanderella the moment she emerged, not Lost but Found, with her own ringed finger held aloft in a salute of imminent matrimony. And then we would perform our vows (officiated by D. Lee), trade rings, and in wedded bliss escape the mall forever.

Even the ghosts seemed excited. They tossed and turned in my guts with such fervour that I had to cling to the counter in order not to go sailing up to the rafters. Meanwhile Gary remained as inscrutable as ever, a picture of stolid dignity between my legs. The faithful steed that Klassanderella and I would ride to freedom.

I laughed aloud. The mall couldn't stop us now!

Well, not so fast. Here was D. Lee—not with Klassanderella in tow, but shuffling out of the shadows with what looked like a shoebox in her arms. Same size, same shape. Brown scuffed cardboard, lid slightly askew. No lover could fit in there. Not a human one, at any rate.

D. Lee settled before me on the other side of the glass. She eyed me, then the box, which she held at chest height, then me again. Are you sure? she asked.

I was indeed, I told her, without conviction. A shoebox portended no joy. Even the shiniest loafers could hardly compare to undying love and happiness.

The lid came off. D. Lee shook out the box on the tray and swivelled it around.

Rings.

Dozens of them, in a heap, identical to my own.

I picked one up, read the inscription: *Now you are mine.*

Another: *Now you are mine* (too).

Another, the very same.

So my ring—my special ring, that icon of affection and adoration and the commingling of souls and the most precious personal intimate extraordinary irreplicable bounteous union that two people could manufacture together, i.e., love, even from a distance of several thousand miles—had been mass-produced. At least forty of the things sat on the tray before me. How many were out there in the world? Another forty? More?

I glanced up. D. Lee met my eyes. So now you see, she said.

My response was only to drop my gaze to my hand. What a pathetic thing the ring seemed now. And what sense did it make to keep it, this meaningless trinket machinated in a factory? In disgrace I removed the ring from my finger and dangled it over the pile—but found that I couldn't let go. Why?

The ring was *mine*.

And here something focused. Like the rack of the camera drawing a scene into crystallized view. I returned the ring to my finger and looked D. Lee dead in the eye.

Sure, I said, out there beyond the confines of the mall perhaps dozens or even hundreds (god forbid, thousands?) of people were strolling about with rings just like this one, deluded in the belief that they and their spouse or partner or paramour were "two in a million" (though even that would mean four in two million, and eight in three million, or 15,200 citizens globally—though more likely at least forty in a million, or 304,000 people total, and perhaps even twice that many, or more).

At any rate, I continued, maybe it was naive to suggest anything special about a relationship based on an illusion, but now that I'd been disabused of said illusion, wasn't I gifted the opportunity to consider my love for Klassanderella, and hers for me, beyond symbols, and *how* our love was unique in less material ways.

Consider the fact that I was living in a mall and she was nursing her ailing mother in the islands, I told D. Lee.

Okay, said D. Lee.

Or the specific ways in which she was mine, and I hers, I expounded, gaining momentum now. How we connected despite Klassanderella's "fun in the sun" childhood and mine of indoor shame. Or the ways in which we made each other laugh—shrill and cackling, with undertones of roar, like a witch hurled over a waterfall. Did any of those other couples with the same rings include one member who was a terrific fishmonger, and another who had, despite suffering a tongue-hair and a rivalry with a sociopathic albeit undeniably talented ponytail, befriended a subterranean pony?

Seems unlikely, said D. Lee.

Precisely! I replied. And, I fairly screamed, never mind that our love thrives despite the literal (watery) gulf between us, traversable only by ferry or flight! A love that one might assume was doomed from the start! And yet we would show them, I told D. Lee; we would show them all!

Here I paused, as my passion had whipped the ghosts into a real lather, and by the time I'd realized what was happening I'd already floated halfway to the ceiling.

Who else would come to my aid but Gary? Gary, that indomitable paragon of loyalty and companionship, as noble a creature as I'd ever met, let alone ridden. Forward he cantered and presented himself to be mounted. The ghosts stilled as I nestled atop his back. And clung there to his mane with both hands.

I felt D. Lee's eyes on me with fresh inquiry. Had she noticed? Indeed.

So, she began, you're a floater.

Had I a name? A name for this pain? I'd never been anything before, let alone afforded a title that also conferred an identity. (My childhood epithets, "Fecal Face" and "The Broken One," were little more than taunts hurled across my sickbed.) Being a floater,

I assumed, occasioned a set of codes and normalcies. What were they, I wondered from atop Gary's stalwart frame. I smiled at D. Lee, hoping to provoke more information.

But all she said was, You'll need boots, and vanished again into the stacks.

Boots! Of course. I eyed my loafers with disdain. These weren't the footwear of a floater—or was it . . . Floater (capitalized)? The syntax of my new nomenclature notwithstanding, yes, boots. I kicked my loafers away (if only I could burn them!) and sat atop Gary with my stockinged feet dangling. But a socked foot is a sad and childish thing. Vulnerable. Even pathetic. So I took those off too—barefoot now, and brazen, I awaited my boots. (And worried faintly about blisters, and eyed my discarded socks with regret.)

Here was D. Lee, a huge black boot in each hand. With effort she hefted one, then the other, up onto the counter and beckoned me closer.

Gary seemed to understand, and knelt. I eyed the boots from my side of the glass. Rubber, huge, with a single buckle flapping undone.

Diver's boots, D. Lee explained. They'll hold you down.

She spun the grate around. There they were.

Retrieving them from Gary's back required some athletic manoeuvres—sliding, clinging, stretching, grasping, grunting, a frantic sort of scuttle, two more grunts. And the boots were very heavy. Each one weighed roughly, I'd estimate, about ten pounds of Gary's meat. Or, by cut, one full pony leg plus a couple of fair-sized steaks hacked from his midsection. And they were meant to go on my feet!

I asked Gary to fetch my socks—and by god, he did. What a

mind! He bent his head and snatched them with his teeth from the floor, and then he "handed" (mouthed) them to me as a neatly arranged pair.

So: first socks, then boots (a struggle I won't get into), and then I slid from Gary's back to the floor. The ghosts were losing it. But, remarkably, all that came of their mania was a slight jounce in my step—a jauntiness that might have passed for a buoyancy of spirit. Walking was laborious—my feet felt encased in concrete—but at least now I wasn't floating up to the rafters every time I moved.

I told D. Lee thanks.

She told me not to sweat.

I did my best to obey.

But what now? I felt myself at a crossroads.

On one side was D. Lee, with whom I had established an irrevocable connection: she'd revealed great secrets and found me great boots. And then there was Gary, my ever-faithful companion—yet now, did I really need him? I sensed that he at last accepted responsibility for leading me to water and forcing me to drink (ghosts), and that having helped rectify that situation, he would now be content to trot on his merry way.

Sure, save an exorcism I would likely be possessed by these hysterical creatures the rest of my days, which I'd also be forced to slog through in twenty pounds of footwear, and if I were ever chased by anyone or anything (a mugger, a cougar, even a sloth), I would invariably be caught and robbed/devoured before I could unbuckle my feet, release the ghosts and float to safety. But Gary had done his best. I could not fault him for that.

Standing there between these two great allies, I felt it was appropriate to make a speech—something rousing yet gracious,

the sort of rallying oratory that leads armies into battle or com-
memorates the historically relevant figures of a given age, that is
quoted down through the generations in times of strife and/or
triumph (for humility), that is recorded to tape and played when-
ever, say, someone about to give a speech is in need of inspiration.
So I puffed out my chest, fixed my gaze on a space equidistant
between Gary and D. Lee, and began:

Friends, I spoke, accomplices, helpers, allies. Mammals
cloven-hoofed and bipedal. Mall-affiliates, basement-dwellers,
employees thereof and the logistically unemployable. Those of
you lost, and those of you found. (Here I eyed D. Lee.) Those
of you still searching. (Gary.) We are all so much small change
in the pocket of god, if we imagine god's kingdom to be this mall
and its various subterranean levels, and god him- or herself to be
the weird overseers that run the security cameras and pen letters
of acceptance to its residency programs and decree a baffling
rubric as to how one's time should be spent there, viz. "making
work" and "engaging the public." But small change accumulated in
a large jar, over time, eventually accrues to an amount adequate to
buy something pretty decent. And together we are pretty decent.

(Here I looked around, nodding, and paused to let the full
effect sink in.)

Sure, I continued, I could walk, one plodding and ridiculously
ballast-encumbered step at a time, out the door of this room, literally turn my back on you both, even "flip you the bird," and never
see either of you two beautiful souls again. But what kind of person
would I be then? (Rueful chuckling.) A bad one. An ungrateful
one. The sort who probably deserves to be torn apart by buzzards
or humiliated by cats. Or shredded in a thresher. Instead I offer you

this: an opportunity. Think of it as a hand extended. That is, think of it not as a hand extended at arm's length, palm out and fingers slightly splayed in a *stop* gesture, then the fingers turned down and flicked thrice in a sort of shooing motion, as if brushing crumbs from the shoulder of an imaginary jacket. No, this extended hand is an invitation. (I extended my hands, one toward Gary and one toward D. Lee.) Come. Come with me. Let my truth set you free.

(Neither the pony nor the clerk made a move. I assumed they thought I was being rhetorical, such was the stunning and, dare I say, humbling effect of my words. So I lowered my hands and gave them more of what they so clearly craved—more speech, more wisdom, more earth-shattering oratorical power.)

Yes, friends, I *intoned* (I was certainly intoning now!), the three of us together will become what I alone cannot: a threesome. For three is stronger than one. Take bones, for example: take any old femur and bend it to its breaking point and the thing will snap in half like a twig. But stack three together? Harder. You'll break your own hands just trying. So imagine us as those three femurs bundled together, unbreakable, resolute and stalwart. If we were an actual leg nothing could stop us—we'd be that tough.

(I looked from Gary to D. Lee and back again, eyes blazing with righteousness.)

So what do you say? Will you join me?

D. Lee put up her hand.

Yes, I said, you there, behind the glass.

Just a question?

Please.

Join you . . . in what?

Why, I said, join me in . . . *overthrowing the mall.*

D. Lee looked aghast. She told me that the mall was where she worked. How she won her bread. If we overthrew it, what then? Who would sign her paycheques? Me?

Me? I said.

Who did I think I was, D. Lee demanded, to try to take that away from her? Me, some blithe and feckless stranger breezing peripatetically through the mall. To think I'd taken advantage of its charity only to deem the place unworthy of its current leadership and worthy of overthrow! And say my rebellion succeeded, said D. Lee, what then? My residency was scheduled to end in a scant two weeks. So off I'd go, leaving the mall in disarray and upheaval in my wake. That is, she added with a cynical laugh, if I were even able to put my scheme into action.

This word—*scheme*—made me twinge. Of course there was no scheme. Only a vague instinct, a sense of disrepute that my inclinations toward propriety resisted. I worried that I'd allowed personal vendettas to overwhelm my senses. Certainly Mr. Ponytail was due for comeuppance. But the whole mall? What would I do, burn it to the ground?

While my mind rambled through these thoughts, D. Lee continued, seeming less offended by my suggestion than exhausted. I felt like a schoolchild being scolded by a beleaguered headmistress—*you shan't lick your classmates' things!*—and, inhabiting the role of the unruly child, I tuned her out, her admonishments washing over me in a formless mist. Meanwhile I fixed my eyes on Gary: would he "be mine" still, despite everything?

The answer seemed to be no. Even my trusted steed was edging away—toward the elevator, shockingly, to flee my presence for good. The speech I'd delivered with such passion and fervour—and a flailing of hands that I'd believed to be the hall-mark of effective oration—had convinced no one. In fact it seemed to have achieved the opposite effect—that is, convinced them only of my lunacy. My former cronies were now "jumping from my ship" and eyeing me with the wary angst of a fellow in a meat tuxedo edging past a hungry lion.

But before Gary could board the elevator, the doors closed and the thing went clanging up toward the main floors of the mall.

I spun upon D. Lee. Her unwillingness to meet my eyes confirmed it: she'd summoned someone. Perhaps with a hidden button or bell expressly designed for such purposes. Betrayed! And of course, as she well knew, my options were to stand heavy-footedly in place in my boots, at the mercy of whoever was intent on my capture, or, unshod, bequeath myself to the whims of the ghosts and float around the room like a stupid balloon. And sud-denly the whole thing struck me as a scheme. Gary, D. Lee: these supposed allies were in fact merely slaves to the mall—of course they'd been planning to turn me over to the authorities.

My god, was that a ponytail tucked up under D. Lee's hat?

My tongue-hair began to twitch.

Grimly we waited for the elevator, the three of us: pony, clerk and whoever or whatever I was supposed to be. A resident? Hardly, as D. Lee had made clear. I was barely a person! And if I'd ever been a floater, I wasn't now, disabled by boots. Though had I ever really been one? Sure, I'd done some floating, but I'd never really got the hang of it, never felt comfortable lofting up in the air, never had much control over where my body gusted. And while the ghosts were still for now, even with the false gravity of my footwear they would still stir to life once I got moving, reminding me again of their control over my whole existence— physically, yes, but also emotionally (since the actual feeling of "butterflies in my gastrointestinal tract" made me just as anxious as the metaphorical version).

There had to be something more that I could say or do as the elevator fetched whoever waited above and began plummeting back to the Lost &/or Found. My speech had come up short—but maybe there was something else to be added, some summation or recursion or rhetorical flourish, that might sway D. Lee and Gary back to my side. But the elevator, I sensed, was nearing, and nothing came to mind. I could only wait—for whom? Judge, jury, executioner. The powers-that-be. A demon or a god. And whatever punishment they had planned for my insolence.

D. Lee stood on the other side of the glass, eyes on the elevator doors. She wouldn't meet my gaze—understandably, I thought. Betrayal is embarrassing. I mean, I felt embarrassed that I'd betrayed her, or tried to, or at least overestimated the depth of our allegiance to one another. And she'd "told on me" and occasioned some sort of, no doubt, even more humiliating fate. Never mind what was almost certainly a ponytail flopping freely from the back of her cap and over her shoulder.

The elevator dinged. My judgment had arrived. Gary withdrew against the wall. In my peripheral vision, I sensed D. Lee retreating into the stacks.

The doors opened. I squinted: blackness, shadow. The elevator was . . . empty.

No, that was not the case. It was teeming—teeming with hair. Hair gathered into ponytails. A thousand ponytails or more. And here they came, a vast and seething army, ropey and squirrelly and galloping one over the next, flowing upon and over me, suckling onto me like leeches, grasping wherever they could—one over my eyes, another over my mouth to muffle my screams—and dragging me into the elevator.

The last thing I sensed before everything went black was a faint, disturbed whinnying from the Lost &/or Found. Through the haze, swimming at the edges of consciousness, I peered out into the room and met Gary's eyes. He surged into the middle of the room, and as the elevator doors were closing he reared back on his hindquarters, forelegs pawing the air, and snorted and neighed.

A cry of solidarity, I felt, as the ponytails closed over me completely.

A gift.

A last, triumphant glimpse of liberty before I was dragged back to the surface, my insurrection was quashed, and my life of subordination, servility and duty resumed as before.

PROGRESS REPORT #7

If there is a creature more noble, more resplendent, more honourable, more elegant and, frankly, more virile than a horse, I wish to never know its name. For there is only so much space in my heart to admire any species other than my own, and that space is currently carved into the shape of a horse. (Try to cram an elephant in there and I'd need an angioplasty.)

Superlatives aside, it is a horse's various utilitarian functions that make it so impressive. Think of all that one can do with, on and to a horse! Ride it, stroke it, go to war atop its back. A horse can deliver your mail. It can swim. It can whinny and it can prance. A human and horse together can compete in a joust or Olympic. Horses can love and they can laugh. They can even be carved into steaks and feasted upon.

Though this isn't a recipe. It's a love letter to horses.

If you are unconvinced of the supremacy of the horse, consider the lowly, moronic cow. As insipid a creature as has ever stalked the earth. Who has ridden a cow? A drunk on a dare, perhaps—right into a ditch. At best! Mount a cow and prepare for disappointment. Cows don't canter. They stare. If a horse ever fixes its gaze on anything, it's to devise a strategy for dominance: "How will I dominate this cow," for example. If nutrition is your pro-bovine argument, beef can be replaced with a dozen things—yak, squab, a clot of beans— and with a confident grip a farmer can milk almost anything.

Have your cow. I'll keep my horse. It was a stupid idea for a trade anyway. How would I get home? While you were galloping off into the sunset, there I'd be hopelessly hitching sleigh to udder. And even when I screamed "Hi-ya!" the cow would only regard me inanely over its shoulder and moo. By the time I'd lashed the thing into motion, you and my former horse would be at home, feet up, sharing a delicious bowl of salt.

Horses are afforded dedicated pastures where they frolic and graze. Such dignity! Especially compared to goats, chewing garbage from the chain-link. Think, too, of the refinement of a stable vs. the putrid squalor of a barn's great bestial orgy, where the ducks and dogs and every species in between (ram, ass, etc.) spend their evenings rutting in dung-matted hay or slurping one another's waste from a trough. Meanwhile the horses are sedately trying on saddles and enjoying a supper of apples and cubed sugar.

And fish? They can't even neigh.

The most sophisticated animals wear shoes: people and horses. No one else! Oh, sure, sometimes you'll catch a monkey trying on a boot—but that's usually just mischief or confusion. It's no coincidence that the horseshoe is a symbol of good fortune. You'd never catch even the most downtrodden loser treating a dog's leash as a luck-suppository—but "there's a horseshoe inside you" is one of the finest compliments you can pay another person.

Since ancient times the horse has helped till the fields, get people where they need to go, and also with logging. One rides into battle atop a stallion; one rides through the dead of night to rouse the blind-drunk veterinarian to deliver another elegant foal. Horses save lives. They make life worth living. To see a horse galloping at full speed is like witnessing god him- or herself streak wildly around a meadow. To hold a horse in one's arms is to feel the pulse of life itself in its purest, cleanest form. To ride one is to dream.

Horses! There's no other animal I'd rather own or love or be.

Also ponies.

THREE

SO THIS WAS THE STATE OF THINGS NOW.

Like a tidal wave carrying me to shore, the ponytails deposited me back in my quarters and then went slithering off into the shadows. An entire day had passed. It was evening. The mall was empty. Desperately I banged out the week's Progress Report, finishing it just in time: K. Sohail arrived, collected it with a rueful look and silently locked me in.

No goodnight.

Cast as I was unceremoniously into the abyss, my sleep was deep but hollow. Eight hours later I found myself hauled up from it, like a corpse from a grave, to a great cacophony of noise.

While my quarters remained locked up and the caretaker was nowhere in sight, the mall was a hive of activity. Drills whined and hammers clapped around the idle chatter that makes such labours tolerable. While I couldn't make out any particular phrases, I imagine the exchanges to have been along the lines of: How's your spouse? Good. Where's your dog? Home. Whom do your children favour? My spouse. What's your favourite colour? Green. Are you lonely? Etc.

As I've mentioned elsewhere and at length, I've never been one to crave the casual camaraderie of the workplace—or the playplace, or any place, really. And yet trapped in my quarters—or cell—I felt palpably excluded by all that transpired outside. What was going on?

With heavy, slow steps I trudged in my boots over to the grating and peered through. The mall was being revitalized: teardowns and rebuilds were underway in all of the nearby stores, and the hallways were lined with pallets stacked chin-high with cling-wrapped boxes of fresh and sundry goods. I craned and peered but couldn't see any members of the mall's new workforce—foremen and/or -women, day labourers, aspiring proprietors, whoever had infiltrated the mall with their vigour and toolkits—at work, as they were, inside all the stores.

But even if I'd spotted one of these dames or fellows, what might I have done from inside my cell? Hailed them cordially? (*Hello, I'm a jovial character who would welcome you properly were I not effectively jailed*—improbable.) Insinuated myself into their banter? I wouldn't even know where to begin! So with a sigh I withdrew from the grating, but not before I noticed, perched on a stool just outside my quarters, the stoic visage of K. Sohail (that is, her entire body, crowned with said visage).

She seemed to be guarding me. From the rigid way she sat, staring straight ahead with the dead-eyed tenacity of a flash-frozen corpse, I could tell that she detected my presence; she just wouldn't acknowledge me. Was it guilt? This was the woman, keep in mind, who for bedtimes upon bedtimes, once upon a time, tenderly—dare I say adoringly—would wish me the sweetest, goodest nights. No longer. Things had changed. No longer my caretaker, she had become my jailer.

I cleared my throat. No response. The woman was a statue. The sounds of de/construction clattered through the halls. I waited some more, and when still she refused to budge, I plodded back to my desk and sat. Rejected. Bereft. And starving: I'd not had any chicken in ages.

What to do but sublimate my sorrows in work? With both of my attempts at insurrection thwarted, maybe it was best to "grind my nose on a stone" and simply perform the role assigned to me. Another week, another Progress Report. Though perhaps an especially strong entry would secure my release; K. Sohail would read its pained and powerful words, recognize her own loneliness, fling open my cage and set me loose like a lobster from its trap. Though instead of pinching her with my talons, I'd gaze into her eyes and tell her, gently: *You are forgiven.*

But what to write? With only two weeks left in my residency, I ought, I felt, to be reaching a conclusion with my "work." If, that is, the two-month term was still in effect after my attempts to overthrow the mall. Perhaps, even as I sat there, the powers-that-be were determining my fate. Maybe I'd be banished. Or, worse still, sentenced to a prolonged stay. Reviewing my Progress Reports to date, they'd identify an impostor who'd failed to fulfill any of the official obligations re "engaging the public" or "making work," and who'd also tried to pull a fast one by bundling said requirements together in the very same Progress Reports.

What Progress had I really made? I'd engaged a woman in an ornately florid hat—that was irrefutable; she'd been rapt. And I suppose I'd engaged Dennis, but our transactional introduction had so quickly developed into friendship that he was barely ever "the public" at all. Also he'd died. I'd engaged Gary, but was a pony "the public"? Unlikely. As employees of the mall, D. Lee and K. Sohail weren't "the public" either—and now the latter wouldn't even engage me with a cursory greeting. I could summarize my alleged Progress thusly: a failed investigation, a failed insurrection, a consumption of ghosts that required remedy by boot, and a humiliating relocation by ponytail mob. And now I was a prisoner in my own (albeit temporary) home.

To make matters worse, my rival evinced an innate mastery of the residency and its requirements. How did Mr. Ponytail go about "engaging the public" and "making work" so naturally? The dastard simply seemed built for it, so much so that he'd reached cult status and likely inspired the mall's rejuvenation. Had that been my purpose here too? Maybe my failure to engage some slavering, mindless public had forced the powers-that-be to invite a second resident. But "saving the mall" was not one of the terms in my Acceptance Letter! How was I to have known?

I noticed that I was boring a hole in the Report before me with the tip of my pen. Such was my rage that I'd destroyed a helpless piece of paper! Shamefully I smoothed the page. Though such a loss of control was understandable. Had I known that "making work" was intended to resurrect the mall (as Mr. Ponytail somehow understood implicitly), I would have gone about my residency with a corresponding strategy.

Would I, though? How?

I struggled to think what I might have done differently. Been chattier with K. Sohail? Been more resolute about "making work" that wasn't simply Progress Reports? Eaten fewer chickens? Eaten *more* chickens? Been less obsessive about solving Dennis's murder? Maybe even accepted that, in the course of doing business, any decent mall would suffer a few casualties? And what about Klassanderella? I suspected that I should have thought about her less: surely keeping "one eye on the prize" of our marriage had been detrimental to my performance here.

That was it: I'd allowed my heart to swell too big, to swell for Dennis, for Klassanderella, for myself—and even in certain nocturnal moments for the mall's authoritarian proxy, the enigmatic K. Sohail. The secret to a successful residency seemed to be cynicism and megalomania—the stuff of Mr. Ponytail. After all, I'd helmed no legion of lookalikes birthed in a parking garage and which now thronged the mall, never mind some sort of restoration project to resurrect the mall's former (I assumed) glory.

All I'd done was made one friend, possibly gotten him killed, eaten a veritable barnyard's worth of chickens, produced a few lacklustre and essentially devious Progress Reports, humiliated myself before a pony named Gary, humiliated myself before the venerable D. Lee, and now I sported a pair of ridiculous diving boots that, though imperative to prevent me from floating around like a blimp, limited my movements to a laborious slog.

Sure, if the mall let me leave I'd be returning to Klassanderella with a truly excellent pair of jeans—they hadn't stripped those from me yet—but the jeans, especially when removed from my legs, were hollow. As was a ring, I thought, stripped from a finger to negate one's betrothal. How quickly it might be rendered an empty symbol, like a hula hoop with no kid in it, or a crucifix in a Dumpster.

Klassanderella! Did she fear it too? That love could so summarily turn to farce? Was she down in the islands right now,
scraping scales from a slimy fish or slopping fistfuls of fish innards
into a bin, gazing at her hand and thinking: *This might mean nothing*. Had she always felt thus?

But, I thought, brightening slightly, sitting up in my chair,
splaying my fingers to display the ring, weren't my feelings for
her inspired by her very lack of cynicism? Down in the islands,
after all, one suffered no pinpricks of the soul such as those of the
Lost &/or Found. With no "line" to the outside world, short of
the odd crackling telegraphic line burdened with birds, perhaps
her ignorance occasioned bliss. The oblivious bliss of love.

This was encouraging.

If Klassanderella believed in the ring, and subsequently in "us,"
then why shouldn't I too? Love was a two-way street, after all, and
even if one of the lanes was bunged up with a horrifying accident—
all flaming metal and limbs strewn about in blood-muck—there
was still clear passage in the other direction where a policeman
could steer traffic around the carnage. That was us! Klassanderella
and I were cop and car, passenger and driver, accommodating
pedestrian and local retailer peering through the window of his
gun shop. We were everything. Our love was all there was!

Even the mall couldn't hold us down. Not a love this strong,
which transcended space and perhaps time. A flame so everlast-
ing even the gales of malice couldn't snuff its fire. So what if the
ring was mass-produced? My jeans were too, probably; it made
them no less wondrous. I owed it to Klassanderella not to admit
defeat, to conclude my residency with dignity, to write the best
damn Progress Reports the mall had ever seen, to keep a stiff

upper lip and my head held high—a lip so stiff it risked sloughing enamel from the adjacent teeth, and a head so high it might well dislocate from my body and go bouncing off down the hall.

I jammed the ring triumphantly back onto my finger.

Hope, then, would be my anchor. Or not my anchor but the ballast I would hurl from the ship of my decrepitude and thusly sail off into the sunset of, also, hope. I'd a cause and a goal—and an enemy to thwart: Ponytail. Ah, Mr. Ponytail. I envisioned him, arrogantly traipsing about his quarters, riveting onlookers with another virtuoso routine. But to what end? Sure, the guy could paint. But each painting was merely a sortie to the next, to the next; he was a pusher, pushing the drug of art. An art that stupefied and subdued, turning patrons into mindless devotees and little else.

That's not what art was for! I didn't think so. No, it was likely meant to excite, to inspire, to transform, to challenge, to change— to *engage*. I'd spent so much time at the mall worrying about my fraudulence, when all along the real fraud was the "pomp and circumstances" of Mr. Ponytail, who didn't engage so much as dupe the public. The envy that had long squelched around in my soul began to congeal—into hatred, loathing and a thirst to reveal the guy as he really was . . .

Not a ponytail at all, I thought, sensing myself on the verge of a "good one":

A *phony*tail.

Yes, that was it—a big phony! Also a crook, a liar, a hustler, a swindler, a grifter, a fleecer, a scammer, a con, a fake, a sneak, a wretch, a trickster, a cheat, a charlatan, a rascal, a scallywag, a bandit, a rogue, a scamp and a rapscallion.

And a jerk. A jerk, certainly, but also a fool and a meanie. And a real ding-a-ling and dingbat, wingding, wingnut, nutbar, nutcase and nutjob. A fellow nutty as a fruitcake, mad as a hatter, crazy as a loon, slippery as an eel, blind as a bat, lonely as a cloud, thunderstruck, lightning-tempered, hot-tempered, ill-tempered, intemperate, temperamental, mentally unfit, fit to be tied, tied up in himself, self-righteous, self-important, self-obsessed, self-absorbed, self-possessed, self-concerned, self-indulgent, self-loving, self-interested, self-centred, not worth a cent and senseless as a centaur.

Simply put, he was not very nice. He was unkind, unbearable, unnatural, unacceptable, uncaring, uncouth, a unique piece, a piece of work, a piece of trash, a trash heap, a garbage pile, a flaming pile, a real pill, a pillager, a philistine, a pig in lipstick, a wolf in sheep's clothing, a whale in a dress, a marmot in galoshes, a kook, a goof, a gimp, an imp and a simpleton.

He was shady too, and shadowy, but also beyond the pale. And irritating. And annoying. And grating, though not so great, more of a degenerate and a reprobate—and a nitwit, a twit, a tit, a boob, a glans, an anus, an ass, a donkey, a chicken, a dog, a leech, a shrimp, a toad, an ape, a baboon, a monkey, a worm, a maggot, a rat, a snake, a pig, full of bull and bull-headed. Though also a blockhead, a pinhead, a dunderhead, a muttonhead, a bonehead, a meathead, a butthead, a knucklehead, a numbskull, a skuldugger, a scumbag, a dirtbag, a bag of hammers, a bag of nails, nails on a chalkboard—Mr. Ponytail, I mean.

While we're at it, he was disgraceful, dishonest, disreputable, disappointing, despicable, a despot, a tyrant, a cutthroat, a murderer, a killer, a bandit, a villain, a felon, a sociopath, a psychopath, certifiable, certified and a stooge, a chump, a sap, a sucker, a patsy, a flunky, a dupe, but also cocky, immodest, arrogant, insipid, bizarre, uppity, snotty, haughty, dotty, pretentious and a pretender.

And guileless yet full of guile, feckless yet full of feck, shiftless yet shifty, affectless yet affected, baseless yet base, shameless yet shameful, bloodless yet bloody, headless yet heady, footless yet afoot (at something), good for nothing, bad to the bone, best ignored, worst ever, mediocre, mundane, unexceptional, exceptionally awful, awfully terrible, terribly horrible—and just really, really bad.

But let's not forget icky, gross, grotesque, gruesome, vile, a live wire, a deadbeat, a birdbrain, a featherbrain, a harebrain, a scatterbrain, cold-hearted, dead-hearted, black-hearted, evil-hearted, heartless, gutless, yellow-bellied, liver-lipped—oh, and the mouth on him! Not to mention toothless and fork-tongued, nosey, cockeyed, hard of hearing, hard to like, easy to hate, high and mighty, lowbrow, middling, upside down, stuck-up, up his own, on the take, full of it, running on empty, a brick shy, a card short, a sandwich less, a bit much and a bridge too far.

Oh, I could go on . . .

But I'd riled myself into a real lather, champing at the bit (Gary!), ready to strike.

First, of course, I'd need to scheme a way out of my quarters.

SOMETHING PHYSICAL WAS CERTAINLY OUT. I wasn't much for exertion anyway, though my mental faculties were admittedly limited as well. It's not like I could telepathically bend the steel bars of my cage or liquefy myself and pour juicily down the halls. I'd no knack for witchcraft. What I did possess, I felt, was the skill of coercion—particularly that manipulative brand rooted in pity. I was quite adept at exploiting my inadequacies to trigger the mercy of others, to get what I wanted by showcasing all that I lacked—because I was weak, because I was ineffectual, because I couldn't achieve anything on my own.

If I'd a war cry, surely it was: *A little help, please?*

Whether people were moved to empathy or sickened into action by this sort of thing was beyond me. All I knew was that an obsequious, cloying, faintly tragic approach was often "the ticket"—or at least my ticket, viz. my ticket to ride, viz. my ticket to ride the wave of someone else's competence to triumph. Or if not triumph, then at least adequacy. Yes, that was it: the safe harbour of adequacy. And in this case, adequacy meant the basic freedoms accorded to human beings under various charters and declarations, such that they weren't caged like some primal beast or quarantined sicko.

What would be my ploy? It needed to be really pathetic. Something feeble and helpless—the emotional equivalent of a weeping baby dangled over a chasm. (If not the imminent peril, it's the discordant shrieking that causes the would-be hero to act.) Something equally annoying, yet something that also compromised my adult dignity. It wasn't exactly compassion I was after, but more that human distaste for humiliation—the way when one sees a dead dog in the street, one doesn't just leave it there, but kicks it under a bush so no one else has to witness the ignominy. My scheme needed to be irritating, ingratiating and embarrassing, yet relatable—and something primal that spoke to the basic functions of human existence . . .

By Jove's eureka! I had it!

Hunger.

I'd not eaten in—now that I was taking stock—days. Who wouldn't share my pain?

Yes, that was "the ticket." A successful scheme had to be rooted in truth. I was an even less proficient actor than I was a hero, so the marrow of my ruse had to be slurped from lived experience. And I was very hungry. I thought I'd long ago exhausted my appetite for chicken, but now the prospect of nibbling a wing had me fairly clucking. While K. Sohail's professional decorum likely inured her to my tricks, there was a group of mall workers who performed their duties with much less vigour—in fact, with a kind of beleaguered suffering—and who might well, if not fall victim to a scheme, at least abet one through their apathy.

Who? Why, the chicken-roasting teens!

But how to contact them? They were way down the hall in the food court. Roasting away. Spearing, hacking, serving. Gamely intercoursing with the public, trading cash for bird, providing nutrition to the hard-working hordes who were remaking the mall. Oh, those teens. I loved them a little, suddenly. Not as I loved Klassanderella. Certainly not! No, this was more a fraternal or sisterly love. As one might love one's lifetime bus driver or a friendly, slinking kitty. I would pet a teen on the head and say, *There*. In the smile I lavished upon them would be affection, admiration—and little to no desire.

Would this help, this new-found warmth? This sudden humanization of a group whom I'd long regarded as little more than automata, and as divorced from sentience as the chickens themselves? I closed my eyes and tried to summon one through clairvoyance. *Teen*, I thought. *Teen!* I opened my eyes. Nothing. The hallway was as empty as ever, aside from K. Sohail's sneakered foot sneaking into view. Tapping twice. (A code?!) And sneakily retracting.

And then, by some divine miracle, it happened: a teen appeared before my quarters with a takeout tray. I rocketed to my feet—though the boots held me fast as concrete blocks. K. Sohail rose, keys out. The grating was unlocked. The kid approached with my lunch, piping hot. Quickly I scrawled a note on the corner of my most recent Progress Report, tore it loose and snuck the note into the teen's fat-spattered shirt pocket.

Amid this exchange, I was enveloped in a bouquet of grease and adolescent hormones: like deep-fried laundry, or a damp sausage. As hormonal and moist a smell as any I'd encountered.

My god, these creatures were alive in a way I'd never be! And yet so constrained by the strictures of their profession: arrive, spear, roast, hack, serve, bill, repeat. If someone set them free, who knew the feral heights to which they'd scuttle. What an army they'd make with me as their leader—with them as my ponytails, scrabbling along behind. An army of me and some teens!

I could only hope that I'd worded my note rousingly enough.

The teen headed off, I dug into my lunch, and K. Sohail locked me up wordlessly once again. As I ate, I fancied myself a sort of dissident unjustly imprisoned. But I'd flung a lifeline into the ether—and who knew, perhaps a teen would snatch it up, haul me to freedom, and the revolution would be at hand. A revolution sustained by chicken, hope and tea (iced or regular).

What was in my note? you ask. A bribe?

Perhaps a bribe; perhaps the promise of a bribe. But in times of desperation one must act accordingly. (Desperately, that is.) So that night, after finishing the lunch leftovers that constituted my dinner, I bedded down and listened as the bustle and clamour through the mall calmed and stilled and people made their way home. Since I was already locked in, at some point K. Sohail simply headed off on her own merry way—though "merry" isn't the right word to describe K. Sohail's movements. Officious, yes. Efficient. Certainly capable. But, no, she wasn't "merry."

If anyone in the mall was merry, it was the mercilessly merry Mr. Ponytail. Though there was a malevolence and arrogance to his merriness, like a cocky, drunk Santa Claus performing sleight-of-hand tricks with a switchblade. He moved with a buoyancy one might mistake for joy, buffeted by hubris rather than a lightness of spirit. In fact, in terms of sheer buoyancy, I certainly had anyone beat: take off my boots and I'd float to the moon. Though there was no joy in that, either. Only ghosts.

By the by, by this point, as with the hair in my mouth, I'd grown accustomed to the ghosts in my guts, and only in passing— actually, while visiting the toilet between lunch and dinner—did I feel them stirring and wondered if a bowel movement might hasten their expulsion. Alas. No luck. Apparently the things were housed in my soul rather than, say, my duodenum. Which meant that I couldn't even abort them by Caesarean section.

My point here is that I'd come to tolerate the ghosts. Sure, every now and then I'd feel them sloshing around between my liver and kidneys. But consider those who live with the pains of dysentery, or the sorrow of a broken heart! I suffered neither— especially not the latter. I was soon to be wed to the love of my life, the woman of my dreams, the ringmate of my ring: Klassanderella.

First, of course, I had to escape.

WELL, THE DAYS PASSED, the renovations continued apace, and I remained locked in.

A teen came in the late morning with my rations of chicken products and tea, refusing to meet my eyes. If there was some sort of clandestine signal coded into how the tray was placed before me, or how the chicken was arrayed atop its leaf mattress, I couldn't say. It didn't help that I couldn't tell one teen from the next—the same shifty gaze, the same disillusioned slouch, a uniform oily, glandular reek. Was this the one to whom I'd given the note? Or was that the one from yesterday? Or were those two in fact *the same one*? How many teens worked in the food court anyway? Four? Forty?

Of course the security cameras were lording over our every exchange, so I could appreciate the teen's/teens' hesitancy to "make a move." It's not as if I were the picture of courage, whittling chicken bones into spears and plotting my escape with tea leaves. No, I'd compliantly been making the week's work as always. And while I ended up ditching that Progress Report, I will include it below—again, as a record. Ultimately, for reasons to be revealed, it became frivolous and self-involved. Yet there is truth in it. Here:

If the eyes are the windows to the soul, then the feet are certainly the gateway to a path that slithers up the legs, plunges into the anus and winnows its way through the intestines before joining up with whatever entered ocularly in some central soul-housing locale. (The spleen? Probably the spleen.)

Like the eyes, feet need lids. You can't just tramp about bare-foot, not through all that glass and syringe! In advanced cultures, podiatric lids are known as footwear—from the barbaric sandal to the devious athleticism of sneakers. Elegant ladies and bold gents totter about on stilettos. Some folks opt for clogs, others slippers, still others ruthlessly bind their feet until the metatarsals crumple like wet paper—and it's beautiful. Detectives wear shoes of gum; a "soft-shoe" is sported by lords of the dance. Children are shod by their parents' decree, be it with roller skates or, hilariously, a single mitten. And while many, if not most, would consider the mighty loafer the height of footwear supremacy, the finest shoes of all are in fact: boots.

My word, a boot can do anything! Tromp, for example. Or stomp. Much heftier and more menacing than any shoe; one can step free from a boot and shake it aloft to deter an attack. And that's not all. Simultaneously you might employ the matching boot to shelter a bird that's been guzzled into a jet engine and regurgitated in a ghastly blizzard of feathers and blood; the boot transforms into a sort of "bird's house" wherein you nurse the ruined creature back to health, dribbling nectar into its beak and splinting its wings with spent pens. Months later you set Colleen free—out to sea, where, fully healed, she sails right into the waves, never to be seen again.

What of it? You've still got your boots.

Boots reduce snow to nothing, every flake mercilessly crushed in their tread. Mud, same: you plow through it like a human tractor, eyes on the prize of wherever you're heading, whether it's a boot buyers' convention or Boot Expo or a support group for the bootless, which you run sensitively, trying to convince a roomful of inferiorly shod lesser lights that one day, with practice and prayer, they might join the booted elite too.

Of course, boots are no monolith, like "fruits" or "the mall." There are as many styles of boot as there are ways to worry a child. For starters: the deadly cowboy boot. Featuring spurs that jangle and high heels, these are not recommended for novices, pretenders or, for example, waterskiing. Only the most experienced boot wearer should dance with the devil in a pair of cowboy boots, lest you want to meet your maker at "the crossroads," i.e., some weird demon intent on stringing his banjo with your guts.

(N.B. Rain boots, contrary to their name, are made for avoiding wet weather. As such, wear them only on the sunniest day of the year. With nary a cloud in the sky, you'll never have to worry about moisture rotting your toenails and peeling them away like dead petals in the wind.)

There are also ski boots and workboots and steel-toed boots and hiking boots and jackboots, to name a few. Also combat boots, desert boots, moon boots, ankle boots and even booties, which are tiny, tiny boots for infants that are in adolescence traded for a saucy pair of go-go boots to be worn until and during the recipient's "first time." Then one commits to a set of grown-up boots all the way to the deathbed, when they're plucked from the bloated corpse, boiled and eaten by one's progeny. You've heard the saying "They died with their boots on"? What's left out is: "Delicious!" In certain cultures.

Tired of your boots? Just reboot. Done with those? That was quick, but no matter. There's an endless supply of boots for even the most erratic enthusiast. No judgment here! Once you're "in," you'll never be "outed" again. The booted, like any community, are as dedicated to fostering kinship and harmony among our ranks as we are to barring undesirables from admission. For not just anyone is worthy of boots.

Say you're the sort to putter about gazing at the heavens and pondering the infinite mysteries of the cosmos—what a waste boots would be, you flighty lunatic. Or say you're an amputee. With all due respect and thanks for your service—whatever and however you served—what good would even one boot do you, really? By all means stuff a pair onto your hands and clomp about the tabletop, whinnying like a mule. But is that what boots are for? Theatre? No. They're for leading the finest human specimens, one sure-footed step at a time, a little bit closer to god.

The teen handed over my food, as always, and left. "Same old," as they say; "same old." To be honest, my life wasn't much different from how it had been for the preceding several weeks, excepting that I took my meals at my desk rather than in the food court. I woke, performed my morning toilet, ate, "worked," ate, "worked," ate, performed my evening toilet, went to bed, woke, and repeated the previous day's activities. While my morning routine included a dutiful tongue shave, the hair seemed in hibernation—dying, I hoped, rather than simply biding its time for a full-on bloom.

At any rate, between "making work" and my steadfast routine, I might have been content to serve out the rest of my time without mutinying at all. Yet I couldn't help but feel that I was being

held against my will, and, as an ostensible "freed spirit," that irked
me. This was no longer a residency. To reside suggests leisure,
perhaps a hammock. Certainly, at the very least, the capacity to
come and go as one pleases. This was a sentence. This was jail
time. This was "the big clink," confirmed again now by the big-
gish clink of K. Sohail's keys turning in the lock. I shuffled over
to my desk, sat down and began to consume my breakfast.

Yet my mind churned wildly, suffocating my appetite. Having
behaved outrageously, I feared that I'd be imprisoned here forever.
And then what? Would I become a sort of zoological curiosity,
with mallgoers and Ponytail acolytes stopping outside my cell to
marvel at the would-be dissident in captivity? Or perhaps I'd
merely offer a cautionary tale to future residents: obey or suffer.
You don't live in the mall; the mall lives in you.

Well, not on my watch, or listen. I couldn't die here, I thought,
twisting my ring around my finger. I had a wedding to get to.
Klassanderella and the dream of our reunion (metaphorical; my
actual dreams were mostly of ponytails—ponytails by the mil-
lions, suffocating me in my sleep) kept the spark of revolution
alive. Oh, and Dennis. Poor guy. Shame about his murder; if in
escaping I might also wreak a little justice, so be it.

I looked up sharply from my desk, casting my gaze toward
the other "woman in my life," out there in the hall. K. Sohail was
a prisoner now too—imprisoned by the task of imprisoning me.
What a waste, squandering her formidable skills as a caretaker.
Who, in her absence, was carting off bags of hair or performing
"rounds"? K. Sohail wasn't taking care of anything—not even
me. She only dwelt in guilty silence outside my door, permitting

the teens to bring me food, then locking me up again. A real caretaker might come in and rub my feet or sing me to sleep. Or, at the very least, wish me goodnight.

K. Sohail hadn't wished me goodnight in weeks.

Weren't we both victims of the mall? If only I could tell her. I leaned toward the hallway and called her name—or its first initial, since that was all I knew. Though I might as well have been chanting *J! J! J!* or *D!* Certainly if someone were hollering a single letter at me, it likely wouldn't inspire me to action, like a cur at a whistle or a whale seduced by the ballads of its barnacle-slathered lover. So I quickly gave up repeating *K* through the bars when, after several minutes, I still hadn't roused her from her post.

I had to have faith that my note would do the trick. That the teens were assembling nightly after the mall closed, in a back alley or graveyard, poring over it and plotting how best to liberate me and set my revolutionary scheme, such as it was, in motion. That morality—or that breed of morality hastened by a bribe—would prevail. That our hatred of the mall was equal and together we would *take it down*.

Did the teens hate the mall, though? Or were they just morose? Hard to tell. We ought to have found solidarity in the mall's rejuvenation: as my singularity had been supplanted by Mr. Ponytail, their food court supremacy was threatened now too. But this assumed that they found their chicken work rewarding. Did they take pride in roasting birds to a golden-brown sheen? Perhaps nourishing hungry patrons sated some instinct of which I was ignorant—ignorant, that is, of such an instinct, as well as of the teens' capacity to care for anyone other than themselves.

But did they even care about that? Themselves, that is?

Certainly one's self-regard begins with basic hygiene, which they seemed to disdain in even its most lax iterations. I was no paragon of egoism, but at least I washed. The teens . . . well, suffice it to say that soap was something with which they had at best a casual relationship. And my fate was in the grubby hands of these youngsters!

All this angst and uncertainty made it impossible to eat, so I set my breakfast aside and turned to the week's Progress Report with a sigh. For the cameras I needed to behave deferentially. The powers-that-be at the mall could never know the fires of insurrection that sparked in my soul. No, all they'd see on their monitors was a defeated has-been, hunched and scribbling away.

But then I noticed something on the napkin folded at the edge of the tray. I picked it up, pretended to wipe my mouth: a message was scrawled on the napkin's underside—a single word, but one that roared like a battle cry.

Okay, said the napkin.

Okay, said the teens!

To my note, my call to arms, they'd taken their sweet time, no doubt, but ultimately responded in the affirmative: *Okay*. Okay! That *okay* struck me as in direct communion with my— and Klassanderella's—ring. A call-and-response—

Me: *Now you are mine.*

Teens: *Okay.*

—in which "mine" implied the collectivity of guerrilla-style warfare rather than the proprietary sentiments of love, and "okay" signified not only an agreement but a commitment to "the cause," viz. our collective freedom from the subjugation and internment of the mall, which we would achieve through militant means and/or trickery and/or simply running away.

Every burgeoning insurrection has no doubt been instigated with a similar exchange—the recalcitrant proletariat trading clandestine communiqués like flirtatious schoolmates in the back of class. But instead of *At recess I shall chase you / Okay*, we were plotting the overthrow of an empire. Or at least committing to said enterprise. A specific scheme had yet to be hatched. Any scheme was, to be fair, still merely an unfertilized egg of agreement bobbing expectantly around our proverbial loins.

(Before I continue, I want to confirm that no impropriety is intended in the above analogy. Perhaps my words got away from me a little. I repeat: my interest in the teens was limited entirely and exclusively to our collective resistance, and not at all romantic, seductive or reproductive. Besides, the teens were repulsive. The thought of even faint proximity to one, let alone bedding down with several of them and their oozing, redolent flesh made the ghosts in my bowels churn queasily.)

So here we were, at any rate. An unlikely army. Me and the teens. In platonic cahoots. I rendered their reply illegible by soaking the napkin with schmaltz and crumpled it into the trash. Nonchalant enough, nothing untoward; it wasn't like the security camera could read my thoughts. Though if it could, I thought, I wondered how many recursions down—how many sub-levels of consciousness—I'd have to descend to escape its psychic purview. Even now, as I was thinking about thinking about what I'd thought, was that far enough? Or did I need to retreat further to dull the seismic echoes of my consciousness from being sensed and read by the camera, or whoever was on the other end?

I could only hope that the mall's mind-reading capacities were compromised by the number of brains suddenly filling its shops and walkways. Surely with the halls teeming with all those enterprising souls, the mall's cognitive receptors would be jammed; it seemed improbable that my feeble notions could rise above the clatter. No, the teens and I were safe—for now. Though tantalizingly it was this very safety that we wished to compromise, to throw great handfuls of caution in the face of the wind, whipping the wind into raging, retributive gales that made our hair dance like snakes and our eyes weep and noses run and ears spout torrents of blood.

But this was no time to worry about windstorms, figurative or otherwise.

It was time to scheme.

Yes, I know I'd "travelled this road before," and my schemes had been mostly ill-fated and ineffectual. But this scheme would be a counter-scheme, an un-scheme and a de-scheme—the ur-scheme to beat all schemes. A scheme by me, executed by teens.

It would begin with a map. A mental map, necessarily, what with the camera peering over my shoulder. Yet as the afternoon progressed my thoughts only spun emptily, like a reel-to-reel recorder that, having reached its end, is reduced to a little strip of flapping tape. I needed to snatch it up, stretch it over the magnets (or what have you) and play the anthem of my freedom, forever. (If only I could charter the parking garage musician— what wasted talent, playing away down there for the cars.)

By the time dinner arrived I'd yet to map or scheme anything, and when the grating clattered open, revealing a teen standing there with a meal tray, I looked away in shame and futility. K. Sohail lingered. The teen approached. We met eyes. I cringed. The teen stared. What a pro! The teens were definitely more practised in the art of subterfuge than I—who knew what they were up to behind the chicken stand. Building a bomb from bones? Maybe they were planning to break me out explosively, the door blown off its hinges and all of us scurrying away under the cover of smoke.

I accepted my dinner. Offered thanks.

Okay, the teen said, shrugged, and withdrew.

Okay! Our code. As K. Sohail locked me in I tried to decipher what the word meant this time, if some particular inflection conveyed that our scheme was moving ahead, whatever said scheme might entail, or even some specific instruction.

But, I thought, picking at my chicken, what could "Okay" possibly mean? Spelled backward it offered no compelling options. My thoughts spun again—that same tape, its loose end snapping and clicking! How to make it play?

I feared the teens were too clever for their own good. Or, more specifically, my good. They seemed to have overestimated me. Perhaps because of my prestigious position at the mall, they'd taken me as some sort of genius versed in everything from boot shopping to cryptology. I could barely crack the codes of basic human speech! Even the most banal social interaction required of me intense concentration for instructive cues: Did someone saying Hi with a particular tilt of their head in fact signify a death wish? Might a stranger's asking for the time really be a desperate confession of soul-wrenching lust? How was one to know, ever, what another person really meant?

Okay, I thought, turning the word around like an artifact, attempting to see it from all sides. *Okay . . . okay . . . okay . . .*

I had a start—a jolt of inspiration.

What if I were spelling it wrong? What if the teens were actually saying *O.K.*? An anagram or initialism, that is, and not a word at all.

So what then might the letters stand for?

Perhaps the *K* signified the *K* of K. Sohail. The only *K* I could think of. The only *K* almost literally at hand. But what about her? Was she the key to our freedom? I needed to figure out what the *O* meant . . .

I rummaged through my vocabulary for *O* verbs.

Occupy? That made no sense. How could one occupy a person? I mean, I could distract her, but was that the teens' big plan? Me creating some diversion while they—what? torched the place? No, their message had to signify something more grandiose than, say, me dancing a saucy jive or feigning anaphylaxis on the floor of my cell.

I thought of other *O* verbs: *order, obviate* (not that I knew what that meant), *ogle, ordain, occlude* (again, no idea), *own, oxygenize, oblige, oil* (surely not!), *outline, open, offer*—none of those made sense.

Observe, maybe? But then what?

Surely not *obey* . . .

And then it struck me: What if the *O* meant . . . *obliterate?*

My god, were those homicidal teens plotting the caretaker's assassination? I sat up, my ghost-clogged stomach lurching. Surely they realized that K. Sohail was only a peon, a pawn, as beholden to the mall as the rest of us. If anything we should be attempting to fold her into our scheme as an ally, not posting her decapitated head on a chicken skewer to portend the revolution.

What would we be then? No better than Mr. Ponytail, surely. And our freedom would be forever stained by an innocent's blood.

I needed to warn her!

But then a second, even more sickening realization came over me. That O.K.—*Obliterate K. [Sohail]*—wasn't simply the teens suggesting a scheme.

They were giving me instructions.

COULD I KILL K. SOHAIL? Probably not. At best in some cow-ardly, distant way. With poison, for example—though a swift-acting brand, nothing that would prolong a painful death or send humours gurgling from her orifices. Even if I could manage something discreet, I thought, I still didn't like the idea of taking a life. Hers especially. She'd been kind to me. Sure, I hadn't enjoyed a *goodnight* in a long time, but to be fair I'd been caught sticking my nose, eyes and appendages where they didn't belong. She was only doing her job. We all have our purposes; that's what makes the world go round. Imagine if I failed to file a Progress Report, the chaos that would descend upon us all . . .

A merciless killing couldn't be the answer. And, really, was a revolution so necessary in the first place? I sat back and surveyed my quarters. They weren't so bad. Where else might one be pro-vided three (counting leftovers) square meals a day and shelter free of charge? The bed was comfy enough, the shower hot, and I'd even been assigned my own private security detail. With a slight shift in thinking, the video camera seemed less of an intrusion than a watchful, caring eye. That's it: I wasn't being surveilled but tended to—maybe even lovingly observed, like a parent looming over the crib of a newborn, except also recording hundreds of hours of uninterrupted footage.

The death of K. Sohail would solve nothing. Consider the guilt I'd experienced over Dennis's demise—and that hadn't even been my fault! Let alone my doing. Let alone something I'd schemed with a bunch of upstart teens via coded message and executed ruthlessly under cover of night. Were I to start offing folks how could I live with myself? I couldn't. And I'd be too wracked with shame to do myself in. The only way that I could stand to kill K. Sohail would be if I killed myself first—a paradox. And simultaneously taking us both out—some sort of kamikaze mission where I went careering into K. Sohail in a shopping cart full of dynamite—seemed out of the question. I'd not the courage for that. Nor the aim.

So what was my aim? I began pacing, the camera tracking me from above. What did I really want? Sure, it was a little lonely in here, a little incapacitating, but my life outside the mall was no great shakes. I found myself twisting my ring—and recalled again my beloved. Klassanderella! How could I keep forgetting her? I suspected that the mall was using sensory deprivation and emotional isolation to "break my heart." But love was stronger than psychological warfare. Especially my love.

I strode to the grating. Called forcefully to K. Sohail: not just her first initial, but her surname too this time.

She rose from her stool. Approached with a quizzical look.

Let me out, I demanded. I've had enough of this tomfoolery, trapped like a cur in a pen. This is no way to treat a person, I told her.

I have an Acceptance Letter. This is unacceptable. Let me out, I say, I said. How can you expect me to engage the public while locked in here? How do you expect me to make work without the thrill of striding about the halls on my own two legs, even in weighted boots? A constrained body is a constrained mind. I've only one week left here. In that week my work should culminate, not be drowned like a guttering candle in a bucket of flame retardant froth! (I was really on a roll now.) Sure, I've made some mistakes, K. Sohail. But haven't we all? Has your curiosity never got the better of you? Led you to wander when you should have only wondered? But what happens when you lock someone up, K. Sohail, is that the mind can *only* wonder, and wonder becomes wanderlust, and someone usually ends up dead. (Here I had to wipe some spittle frothing at the corners of my lips; I was in an actual lather!) Is that what you want, K. Sohail? Another body on your hands? No, just a glimmer of freedom would salve my churning soul. In here all I can think of is murder. Murder, murder. But let me loose, let me breathe, let me share the air with my fellow mall-dwelling men and/or women, and my spirits will ignite with the fires of empathy. I will look the public in the eyes and see straight into their hearts—and I'll see goodness, K. Sohail. My bloodlust will be quenched by feasting not literally but figuratively upon the hearts of strangers. I will become a person again. I will be fully alive. I will live. (Here came the climax.) I am failing to live, K. Sohail. A person must live! Live while they can, as fully as they can. Live! So let me out, I beg you. Set me free. Let me live. Let me live!

And K. Sohail, bless her, simply shrugged, produced her keys and released me.

The mall was unrecognizable. Everywhere the stores were under renovation, teeming with men and women, some in hard hats, others in neon vests and a few with the officious aura of the tycoon in exquisitely tailored pantsuits. The halls reverberated with whining power saws and pattering hammers. Signs were coming down and new ones were going up. The hair salon had been transformed into a jeweller; diamonds glittered in display cases where the barber chairs had been.

Struggling with the heavy steps of my weighted boots I trudged the halls, feeling like someone awoken from a decades-long slumber to a world of incomprehension. An alien, an intruder. All these people were real, while I was little more than a spectral entity shimmering through their dreams. No one paid me any attention. If the mall's new proprietors were my public, engaging them would have involved storming up, grasping someone by the lapels and screaming into their face. Less of an engagement than an assault. And I was already treading on thin ice; K. Sohail trailed me at a distance, like a warden whose prisoner has been afforded a final stroll prior to execution.

Also of note were posters pasted everywhere. *MADNESS SALE*, they proclaimed in a hysterical font, and then there was an illustration of someone losing their mind. Alongside a constellation of dollar signs circling the figure's head, the impending madness was conveyed with loosening spirals meant to indicate unhinging of the brain. The eyes were crossed too, a classic depiction of derangement, while the feet were pointed inward as with a shameful pigeon or cowardly skier, and the arms flailed maniacally as though batting the dollar signs away—or trying to snatch them.

At the bottom of the poster was a date, one that struck me as familiar. I squinted: the Madness Sale was scheduled for the final day of my residency. Coincidence? Probably not. Though possibly. It wasn't as if I was the hub around which spun the mall's wheel of commerce. Yet I still detected a whiff of conspiracy in the air, something nefarious that lurked beyond my purview and threatened me with potential (further) humiliation. Was the Madness Sale simply another scheme to degrade and diminish me?

In fact, as I examined the poster plastered to the wall by the former hair salon, I began to sense that the figure depicted as the harbinger of madness did in many ways resemble yours truly. To be fair, I did walk with an inward slant of my toes, and while I haven't confessed such a thing in these pages, I have often found myself swatting at things that aren't there. Also the spirals had the look of stout and curly hairs—one of which seemed to be springing from the figure's mouth. (At this realization my own tongue-hair roused itself for the first time in days, piercing up through a taste bud and cilially toying my gums.) Yes, I thought, biting down grimly: the illustration—a man alone, mind unhinged, ineffectual and grovelling—captured something intrinsically my own.

And, examining the poster even more closely, I realized that what I'd at first taken for a splash of ink or an ornamental curlicue in the bottom corner was in fact the artist's signature. I probably don't have to clarify who it was—what foul and devious creature had inked and possibly plotted the whole affair— though I will, just for the sake of thoroughness: *Mr. Ponytail.* (Of course it was! Who else?) His autograph stung like a slap across my cheek.

So. A final showdown. I imagined the Madness Sale as an auction for my soul—me up there "on the block" with Ponytail caterwauling at breakneck speeds in an attempt to entice the highest bidder, pounding a gavel, detailing my various features with a sardonic, mocking tone. Of course, per his irony, there would be no bids, just a dull and vacuous silence that settled over the crowd. I would go once, go twice and not be sold, and as such banished to the Lost &/or Found, locked away by D. Lee in that great trove of forgone and forgotten things.

I realized that someone was standing beside me. A presence looming at my shoulder. A faint mortal odour. A whisk of the wind of human breath.

I turned, slowly, with dread.

And nearly fell to the floor.

Standing there, equipped once again with a luxuriant ponytail and grinning magnificently, was Dennis.

Well, it was Dennis, but it wasn't Dennis. Something was off. The smile seemed painted on, with none of his characteristic exuberance animating it. The eyes were without light. Even the way he stood struck me as lifeless, like a mannequin manipulated into a human posture. And he said nothing, just stared at me. God, though, that ponytail was still glorious, gleaming with a kind of inner radiance and flowing over his shoulder like a brook or a stream. Even after all I'd suffered at the hands (or tufts?) of ponytails, I found myself admiring this specimen. It was simply that splendid.

I tried to initiate conversation with a casual greeting. A simple hello, no mention of Dennis's apparent return from the dead. (Or maybe he'd just been swimming?)

But all he did was stare, that weird smile blazing like a signal fire. But signalling what? Or whom? It communicated nothing. It didn't speak to me. The smile was as mute and inexpressive as the man himself. It struck me as a mask pasted over some private torment. Even my gut-ghosts seemed discomfited by it; they churned and fidgeted, and were it not for my boots they would have launched me to the ceiling.

Another tack, then: I asked Dennis if he was excited about the Madness Sale.

He kept grinning.

Yet a glimmer of panic shone in his eyes, and they flicked sideways as if searching for escape. And he wavered ever so faintly, as if buffeted by some internal wind. And then the disturbance was gone. The waxen grin resumed.

The mall's certainly transforming, I said.

Grin.

It was nearly suppertime—would he like to join me? Like old times?

Grin.

Our usual or at least previously habitual routine of a whole chicken, that is: shared.

Grin.

He could have as much leg as he liked!

Grin.

I'd even splurge for his iced tea.

Grin.

Great, then. Should we head in that direction, then, or . . .

Grin.

I took a heavy-footed step toward the food court. And realized that dinner would require a face-to-face encounter with the teens—the teens, mind, who had just encouraged me to *O[bliterate] K. [Sohail]*. Thank god, I thought, that I would have Dennis at my side for support. For who knew the depths of the teens' commitment to "the cause"; should they learn that I wasn't up to the task of murder, perhaps they'd deem me a traitor and as such disposable (literally, like a bag of hair). I wasn't sure if Dennis would be physically capable of preventing an assault, but I hoped that at least the teens would balk at the presence of a witness.

At any rate, good to have Dennis along. The problem, however, was that he hadn't moved. The fellow just stood there with that maddening grin anchored on his face, eyes glazed and distant, ponytail draped over his shoulder. Off we go, I encouraged him, taking another step toward the food court. Nothing: no reply, no sign of motion. Just that grin, less like a fire now than a dying star. Slowly I backed away, announcing that Dennis could take his time, no problem, I'd see him at the food court, maybe go ahead and order for both of us, and how nice it was to have him back in the mall.

Meanwhile Dennis just grinned and grinned, growing smaller as I trod in my boots down the hall with occasional checks over my shoulder. And then, as I reached the turn toward the escalators, I looked back a final time—and he was gone. Only the din of construction filled the empty hall. (Excepting K. Sohail, who skulked about in the shadows, an eye on me as always.) How had Dennis vanished so quickly? Had he been an apparition? It was as if my old friend had evaporated into thin air.

PROGRESS REPORT #8

Living! The thing that gives life meaning. Living is one of the most favourable things about being a person, and a stern head-shake to those misanthropes who believe otherwise. Murderers especially. Though to each his or her own. It's your life. And if you choose to spend it deathmongering, I suppose that's between you and whatever "maker" adjudicates your heaven application. Me, though, I believe it's better to live, not to mention let live, to sniff the flowers of glory, to splash through the brooks of joy, to prance through the meadows of ecstasy with a frisky song in the heart, upon the lips and ringing in the ears like a nice tinnitus.

Life begins at zero. For a while half of you is one place and the other half somewhere else, and the two bits combine during the respective owners' nude frolics. Basically the fishy thing of your soul punctures the orb of your head—and poof: a brain. And soon enough that brain grows some other stuff and you're a weird thing swimming around a lady's guts. Gradually, through a process known as "science," your fins become hands, your gills turn into feet, and your sweeping, flamboyant tail curls itself into a little beaked triangle, locates itself in the middle of your face, and declares itself a nose.

What do you eat in there? Whatever goes passing by. Your frog-like forked tongue can snag anything within a sixteen-inch radius—ova, platelets, raspberry seeds, DNA soup. You name it. Also milk. From the time we're no bigger than a drop of the stuff ourselves, milk is the lifeblood of humanity. Without it we are milk toast, as the saying goes. Toast, that is, soaked disgustingly in milk. And then what? Smeared somewhere. Gross.

After a baby "comes out" things proceed until the first-year anniversary, which is celebrated with terrific pomp and a modest—some say almost undetectable—quantity of circumstance. Things then proceed through a sequence of "birth days" (cakes, flames, puppies in a bag) until you turn, say, fifty or ninety and announce, "Enough!" And instead of a party, you hold for yourself a kind of vigil where the candles burn unblown until the wicks shrivel upon themselves and all that remains is a platter of wax.

When you're living, everything feels good. Even surgery. "No need for an anaesthetic," you assure the dentist while she sharpens her blades. "I'm just going to grin my way through this one." It's that simple. If your soul is boogying and jiving with the power of living, everything else is your dance floor: a delicious celery feast here, a sword through the forearm there. Pleasure and/or pain. It's all just the stuff of life, the yen and zen of living.

What else makes life worth living, or living worth spending a life doing? Why, love! Love is to life as soil is to death, and there's no better way to spend your days than buried alive in love's wormy mud. How many kinds of love are there? At least eight. Spend your life sampling love's generous buffet, and on your deathbed you'll know that every moment preceding your organs' failing and splattering viscera all over the sheets was well spent. Best of all, you'll be surrounded by loved ones to clean up the mess.

Of course, with life comes death, though rarely simultaneously. Instead think of death as the dessert to life's splendid luncheon. Do you dare partake? Well, you kind of have to. It's as if said luncheon were hosted by the devil—it's great that you've gorged yourself sick on all that living, but now it's time to stuff the cheesecake of mortality down your gullet. Served on a pickaxe. And that's precisely what does you in.

A cemetery is one place where the dead are deposited. Another is the sea—what's known as a "watery grave," because of the attendant wetness. Some people get lit on fire; others are wrapped in tissues, stood upright in a box and left for intrepid archaeologists to peel, but never lick. However you decide to discard your remains, what's lost forever is your soul—no matter how thoroughly someone exhumes the body, whether with saws or dynamite.

Is there life after death? By its specific parameters, no. Although there have been reports of the dead "giving themselves a raise" to spook the living or reclaim unpaid debts, whether as ghosts, vampires, zombies or a vaporous, drifting substance akin to the damp stuff of a sneeze.

The point though is: live! Live, damn you. Stop standing around with your head in the shrubs—get out and turn your face to the winds of vivacity. Let it ruffle your hair, flutter your eyelids, winnow inside your orifices and tickle your soul. And then go bounding off to drink life's sweet nectar—from a flower, from the lips of a lover, from a trough being hogged by some hogs. Guzzle away, friend. For soon enough every drop will be all gone.

THE RENOVATIONS WERE COMPLETE. The mall was revitalized. The Madness Sale was imminent. Every store was open for business—or would be. In fact the only shuttered enterprise was the chicken stall. The rotisseries were gone. The cash register had been packed away under a vinyl cover. There was nary a teen in sight. Even the unctuous reek of the place had been scrubbed clean, replaced with ammonia and citrus.

Had the teens' homicidal scheme been thwarted? Had they been punished? Was I, in some way, to blame? Might I be next? Though this swell of fear quickly deflated: if the mall wished it, my time (on earth) would have expired long ago. Now that K. Sohail had set me free from my quarters, as if I'd served some punitive sentence and could now emerge having learned my lesson, my presence in the mall seemed to have been judged so ineffectual that I didn't even require observation. I was beginning to feel toyed with, as if my fumblings at life were mere entertainment . . .

Confronted with a bounty of choice at the food court, from

noodles of various girths and ethnicities to "wraps," I merely approached the nearest kiosk and, as a sort of testament or memorial, asked for chicken—broiled, boiled, fried, chopped to bits and dispersed through rice, chicken on a stick, on a prong, à la mode, you name it. Just give me chicken, I told the uniformed woman in a hairnet. Well, they didn't have chicken. Would squab do? Yes. It would have to.

I took my squab, tenderly poached and accompanied by a small cup of nectar, to my old table. For now, the food court was empty. I could sense the mall readying itself for something grand—like a drunk uncle waddling out at a family function and commanding everyone's attention before flopping to the ground in the pulsations of an interpretive dance. Soon they would arrive, the mall's proprietors, flooding this place by the hundreds. And right behind them would be the massing, maddened public, here for the Sale. It was going to be bonkers. Units would move. Nothing would be off limits. *Everything must go.*

The squab was fine. I returned to my quarters against a tide of shopkeepers (eyes wild, registering my presence only as something to swerve around) arriving for the day's trade, and sat at my desk before the blank page of my final Progress Report—my Final Report, in fact. Minutes turned into an hour and still the thing gaped at me from my desk, vacuous as a yawn. Fatigued with me, fatigued with my existence. What was the point?

Though maybe this was precisely it. Having had the flicker of revolution snuffed so summarily, perhaps the only resistance left was apathy. Taking any sort of action was just playing my prescriptive role at the mall, creating an illusory purpose to chase like a rat in a maze while my keepers jiggered the walls to keep me running in circles. And they laughed. Oh, how I'm sure they laughed.

So who was in charge? If all this wasn't helmed by Mr. Ponytail, he was at least an agent of the mall's deep state. I hadn't seen him in ages yet still sensed his presence, ubiquitous and omnipotent and "pulling the strings," as if each hair in that magnificent bunch tugged about his army of puppets—K. Sohail, D. Lee, perhaps even Gary, and certainly me. Our every action, every gesture and perhaps even every thought were of Ponytail's grand design. But a design for what? Mastery and manipulation? To what end?

Certainly the Madness Sale represented the culmination of some infernal and insidious scheme that had been conceived long before I'd begun my residency. At its finale loomed something terrible—not just a storm but whatever lay beyond the horizon, that horrifying infinitude of nothingness and oblivion. What would be left? Anything?

Oh, wow, here was K. Sohail, squeaking and jingling up to my quarters.

Good morning, I said. (Boldly, I thought.)

She offered me a forlorn smile. I was surprised to hear her speak: You're nearly finished here, she said.

I told her, Indeed. (Though, I wondered, was she talking about my residency or the collective fate of us all? And by "here" did she mean the mall—or the *planet*?)

She seemed poised to say something else. Not goodnight—now was hardly the time . . . I waited. What would it be? A warning? An affectionate send-off? An apology?

Instead she simply stared. I sensed in that lingering look—god, was it longing? Was K. Sohail "after me"? Being desired was unfamiliar; immediately I second-guessed myself. Weren't the eyes of lust meant to be more hooded, the lips gaping as if for a smooch, the breath heavy and amorous? K. Sohail's face looked sad.

I tried to contort my own features into a mirror of hers. I softened my gaze. I tilted my head to communicate, I hoped, compassion—reinforced by a slight jut of the chin. My nose underwent a subtle scrunch. The eyebrows peaked.

K. Sohail's own expression shifted into bafflement.

Immediately I felt foolish, engaged in a bizarre pantomime that likely conveyed only inner chaos. So I gave up, stood, clapped my hands and feigned enthusiasm—for what? The Madness Sale? It would have to be.

She looked at me for a moment longer and then, with a hunch of the shoulders, seemed to collapse—from guilt? From disappointment? From the invariable withering isolation of a failed attempt at camaraderie?

Ashamed now, I gazed past her into the mall. Where the new proprietors were readying their shops. Shutters were being hauled up, lights were turning on. Display racks were being hauled into the hallways. Music began playing over the public address system—the benign, airy music of the void. Yet it also crackled with anticipation.

It was only a matter of time now. The Madness was about to begin.

THIS IS HOW IT WENT: the mall opened and the doors burst like a fraught dam and in gushed a torrent of shoppers. From my desk I watched them stampede past my quarters. Their eyes were rabid with thrift. Their arms were extended as if to race across some imagined finish line, or to snatch a sale item from a rival. A low roar accompanied them as they thundered through the mall. The roar of their thundering footsteps, to be sure, but also something internal—like the growl of an engine, sputtering and threatening to blow.

Oh: every single person—to the man, woman and child—sported a ponytail.

These ponytails fluttered behind the shoppers like wind-socks streaming in the breeze—in the winds of change. An ungodly legion of ponytails. A terrible sea of ponytails. Flowing, rustling. A conflagration of ponytails, stoked by the Madness Sale, whipped about with the furor of flames. Ponytails, ponytails. So many ponytails.

I had to fetch my razor, my tongue-hair was whipped into such a frenzy. But no matter how resolutely I scraped it through my mouth, the hair kept sprouting up and flailing—in joy, in celebration. In victory.

The crowd didn't relent. Even after the initial surge, the halls remained packed. That great mob heaved as one in and out of the shops, arms loaded with purchases: shoes, boots, microscopic heat-wave ovens, you name it. There was something almost tectonic about their movements, uniform and gargantuan and seismic. None of them paid me the slightest heed, even when I rose to perform some light calisthenics (hopping, stooping, "jacks") in an effort to still the tongue-hair. They were here for deals and I'd nothing to offer them, nothing for sale—nothing to quench their insatiable madness.

What could I do? Hide.

So I hid, contemplating my Final Report. How might I sum up my time in the mall? What had I accomplished, beyond my own dishonour? There had been no culmination of my residency; it had not peaked in some grand display. Nothing like the majesty of Mr. Ponytail's not-quite-seven—and he'd sketched that on his first day! Who knew what feats he'd conjured since. If my Progress Reports comprised my "work," they didn't operate on any kind of trajectory to which now I might append some climax. No—the climax was happening out there in the mall. And it had nothing to do with me.

On the blank page I drew an open circle: a ring.

The tongue-hair writhed against my teeth—wispy as a thread, tugging at the root. If I were to escape this place and enjoy a reunification with my beloved Klassanderella, I'd likely try to have it surgically removed. Our first kiss after so long ought not to be tainted by a foreign body.

I tried to still it by biting down, but still the tip wriggled about like a worm trapped under a spade. And then I felt a snap in my mouth. The thing had broken loose.

For a moment, nothing happened. I could feel it testing its new freedom, swaying this way and that. A pause.

And then, in a great surge, my body began to unravel.

Up through my arms and legs, from a pool in my guts, the hair reeled up my throat in a damp tangle. As my cheeks began to balloon with the stuff, I opened my mouth—and out it came. A great, furry vomit went scrawling down my chin to the floor. And still more followed: flowing up from my fingertips and toes, from deep within organ tissue, from the cells themselves. Rivulets of hair came twisting up through my body and poured out of my face, gathering in a massive knot the size of a beachball at my feet.

From somewhere deep within my brain, some cortex or lobe, I felt the end jerk loose, and out it came too, slurped into that infernal tumbleweed. And then, made whole, the thing sat there for a moment—almost as if it were gloating at me—before it went skittering off into the mall to join that mob of bodies and all their madness.

The shock of this had barely subsided when I noticed the ornately hatted woman standing in the doorway of my quarters. My god! She'd returned—just as I'd hoped. Or feared?

I straightened in the chair behind my desk, assuming an air of enterprise and diligence. Please, I beckoned: enter.

But the ornately hatted woman simply stared. The feather in

her hat seemed to droop. The spray of violets wilted. The bow trailed loosely at its ends, etc. And she seemed, instead of arriving with an agenda or demand, to be stunned into inertia: frozen, as it were, in place. Clearly she'd witnessed my torrential vomit of hair. I had to do something to distract her—quickly. She was my only patron. This was my moment, I sensed. A chance at redemption for all I'd failed to be.

So I rose, slowly, holding her gaze.

And began to dance.

I opened with a subtle two-step. A tap of the toes of my right foot (still in my weighted boots, so this required considerable strength and effort): once to the left, once to the right and back again. My leg elongated. The rest of my body as rigid as a stick.

Next I added a slight dip from the hips. Everything in rhythm. My face expressionless. The ornately hatted woman was entranced. Or at least watching. Perhaps with awe, perhaps with curiosity: How far would this go? Would there be pirouettes?

Well, by god, next I gave her a pirouette.

And then fell back into the toe tap w/rhythmic crouch.

Feeling that something else was required, I lifted my arms slowly over my head, forming a kind of proscenium arch—my quarters were my stage, my body my vessel, the ornately hatted woman my adoring public. With my hands clasped above—still tapping, still crouching—I felt as true as light, and very much like the letter Q. Everything was in synch. I was pure form, pure being. The music that I danced to was the music of my soul. Or, rather, *our* souls—that metaphysical orchestra where the ornately hatted woman's spirit and my spirit sawed and tootled away together, or pounded some drums.

What next? I was running out of moves. I felt now slightly trapped in the pattern I'd established, tapping and crouching with my arms up and struggling a bit to maintain my balance. But I couldn't let the ornately hatted woman down. Not after all we'd been through. Our sacrifices and history. Two months ago she'd been amazed by my work ethic. And now here, at last, was the artistic creation that had emerged from my months of study. A dance to end all dances. How should it end?

The ornately hatted woman held up a hand. Enough, she said.

So I stopped.

Enough dancing, she said. She seemed impatient; her next question rumbled out scratchy and peptic, like a vomit of hair: Do you know what's going on out there?

The Madness Sale, I replied (with confidence).

Oh, yes—*the Madness Sale*, she mimicked. Yes, I suppose that's what they're calling it. No, no, you beautiful fool. I mean what's really going on. What's *happening*. What's happening to us all!

I suppose I had some idea, though I wasn't quite sure how to frame it. At a loss, I tried one of the toe-taps that had so delighted her only seconds before.

The ornately hatted woman waved this away. Save your dancing for a time when there's a reason to dance, she said. Do you know who I am?

I admitted I did not.

Leaning against the doorway to my quarters, she looked over her shoulder at the teeming masses. Turned back to me. Shook her head. Sighed.

I waited.

This mall is mine, she said sadly. I'm its owner. And it used to be a glorious place. A place for a kind of worship. A place to discover what you most wanted and adored.

Yes, I said. (The ghosts were stirred by this too, and they began a dance of their own around my innards.)

I've been watching you, said the ornately hatted woman, indicating the camera above my head. Hoping.

I eyed the camera. And thought but didn't say: *Hoping for what?*

I know you've tried your best, she continued. Considering the circumstances. And certainly, perhaps regrettably, though I suppose it was to be expected, you let your curiosity get the better of you. You saw some things I wish you hadn't. The mall's inner workings can be . . . bewildering, let's say, to the uninitiated. But your discoveries aren't what I regret most.

Here she was interrupted by a roar from the halls—some especially spectacular deal or giveaway had been announced and the crowds were surging with renewed purpose. Toward the escalator, I was certain. And upstairs, toward Mr. Ponytail.

The ornately hatted woman regarded me now with an expression of desolation. You were our last hope, she said, shaking her head.

I?

Yes, you.

But . . .

It's too late now, she said. But thank you for trying.

And with that she released herself from the doorway, wavered for a moment and then fell backward, into the hall, where she was swept up into that tide of bodies and carried away like a bit of flotsam upon a current—one that hurtled headlong to some precipice or chasm where she would be carried over, smashed and ruined on the rocks below.

Except above, i.e., to the second floor, where everyone was going.

I sat down at my desk to take stock.

I'd never been anyone's hope before. Not even my own. (I wondered briefly if I'd ever been anyone's *anything*—short of Klassanderella's beloved, of course, though there was a kind of duty to that.) At first I felt cowed, but gradually I allowed the ornately hatted woman's revelation to embolden me. A stranger's hope was like being garlanded with love, or celebrated as a time traveller to (or from?) a happier future. I gazed out into the mall, into all the bodies into which she might have suicided, and thought:

Perhaps I've not failed the mall just yet.

And thought:

This isn't over.

And:

Vengeance is mine . . . maybe.

I moved to the edge of my quarters and stood watching the mallgoers heave past. I searched for an opening, but they were shoulder to shoulder, packed in as tightly as sailors at a dance, their eyes glittering with covetous hunger. Entering that great thronging mass would be like diving into a lake of hardening concrete: Would I make it? Would it suck me in and ossify me and I'd be forced to live there, among all those bodies, forever?

But then the crowd began to thin—to a gurgle, then a trickle, then a few scant drops, i.e., a man and a woman rushing by in socked feet, a child spinning past in a tutu, and three elderly characters bringing up the rear, lugging walkers with a kind of besieged desperation, haranguing one another to *Hurry up*, though the lot of them were labouring equally.

I slipped in behind them, overtook them, left them "eating my dirt." And tromped in my boots toward the food court, where the crowd was gathering. On the way, I ducked into a brand-new Knife & Blade concern and procured from a counter display—scissors. This was more instinct than scheme, though the moment I held those cold steel blades in my hand I felt their power coursing through me, and I moved back into the mall with weaponized nerves and a new sense of purpose—of, dare I say, wrath.

The crowd filled the food court, assembling at the base of the escalator and spilling into the mall. There were hundreds of people—possibly thousands. (One of my skills is not crowd-size estimation; I am not sure what my skills are.) At any rate, with my stolen scissors secreted "up my sleeve," I pushed through that stinking, seething mass of humanity, many of them clutching shopping bags full of recent purchases and/or coupons for future attempts, and squirmed between elbows and ducked under hats (none so ornate as the ornately hatted woman's, of whom there was no sign) and did my best to avoid all those disgusting ponytails drooping down backs and curling over shoulders like stoles or scarves, until I was at what I perceived to be the "front," with a view straight up the escalator to the upper-floor mezzanine, where Mr. Ponytail would no doubt make his appearance.

I and my scissors were ready.

THE LAST FEW STRAGGLERS ARRIVED into that cone of sunshine beaming in celestially through the food court skylight,
and an expectant hush fell over the crowd. Everything went still
for a moment—even me. Even the ghosts in my belly. All eyes
were on the top of the escalator (inoperative now; simply stairs)
where Mr. Ponytail would appear in full glory, as luxuriantly
splayed and displayed as anyone had ever seen him. Grand-
standing. Showcasing himself like a prize pony trotting out to
the fawning cries of would-be riders.

That wasn't right. Mr. Ponytail was no pony; how insulting
to Gary. Something else. An ass, maybe, that fancied itself some
make of prince. But more monstrous: a twelve-legged zebra. A
scaly dog with wings.

The air prickled with anticipation. Every man, woman, child
and whoever else stood there side by each and frozen-footed (and
-jawed, and -eyed); even their ponytails seemed rapt. I thought I
saw my former tongue-hair, now looking like a rolled-up musk-
rat, go wheeling past. The moment of revelation was at hand, or

close to it—the culmination of the Madness Sale, the climax of Ponytail's tenure and the anticlimax of my own. He would emerge and do something spectacular, and my disgrace would be complete.

But first: something else happened.

Out of the corner of my eye I detected movement. Something brown, shimmying glossily in the refracted sunlight. Before I could make a diagnosis (a wendigo? a bat?), I sensed a similar agitation before and beside me, and also behind, and then everywhere all around.

The ponytails were stirring. (Think ferrets nosing up from their lairs.) Twitching—left, right. This way, that. Swaying. In synch. In rhythm.

My god.

The loathsome things were *dancing*.

I looked into the face of the woman next to me, to the man beyond, past him to a child, and so on. Nary a one seemed to notice the ponytails squirming upon their backs. Had they gone blind? And also senseless? While the ponytails twitched and writhed and crawled, each pair of eyes—save one cycloptic character in a pirate's patch—remained fixed on the escalator for their overlord.

I did not care for this turn of events one bit. There was something a little too gleeful about the ponytails' dancing. (And a bit too uncomfortably reminiscent of my own tantalizing moves before the ornately hatted woman only minutes prior.) I had to resist the urge to grab one of those hair tubes and choke the life from the thing. To wring its neck. Or, I thought, as I tightened my grip on the pilfered scissors, I could just go on a glorious cutting spree . . .

No! Even if I were to take down a few dozen, it would be no good if I were subdued before getting to their leader. *Patience*, I told myself. So I pocketed the scissors, clutched my hands under my armpits and stared sullenly at my feet. If I didn't look up, nothing would tempt me into violence. And surely some insipid roar of adulation would alert me when my rival appeared on the scene: then I could act. Until that moment, I ought to keep my thoughts and actions to myself, I thought, and perhaps simply admire the remarkable girth of the diving boots with which D. Lee had outfitted me—like a smallish submarine on each foot—and ready myself for the real drama.

Besides, for now at least, what did it matter if some ponytails were dancing? A vague irritation, certainly, but it wasn't a threat to me, or a direct insult—perhaps a taunt, but I could handle such things. I always had. Was it really so bad?

It was not.

However, then their human hosts started hissing.

A food court full of *hissing*. What a horrible sound! All those people reducing themselves to the ghoulish sibilance of snakes. A thousand (odd?) tongues pressed to 32,000-odd teeth with however many hundred gallons of air kissed through, the lot of it commingling into a demonic whisper that drifted up into the rafters of the food court and hung there with the eerie quality of a witch-conjured mist. Hissing, hissing, hissing, without cease— without, somehow, breath! Their faces expressionless. Why?

And the ponytails responded to this hissing by whipping themselves into a real frenzy. I couldn't look away now! It was riveting. A crowd so stiff and unmoving and hissing while their ponytails danced about like charmed cobras. And me amid it all:

no ponytail, and instead of hissing reverence, my silence pulsed with intimations of murder. The scissors cold against my leg in my pocket.

The incantatory hissing seemed to be growing louder too, and with it the ponytails accentuated their movements—they were really going for it now, thrashing around with such melodrama and violence that they seemed ready to tear themselves loose from their respective heads.

And still their master had yet to appear.

I decided to make a move up the escalator, if only to escape the hissing masses and their lurid, histrionic ponytails. As I squeezed through that brainwashed horde, some hair brushed me. The ends pricked and needled my skin as if trying to find a way in. By some mercy I reached the bottom stair unscathed, but as I went to step aboard, both sides of the thing—up and down—came alive, plummeting in opposition to my ascent. Thanks to my earlier dancing for the ornately hatted woman, I was feeling limber: some indoor mountaineering presented a welcome challenge.

And so, in my weighted boots, I began to climb.

The hissing increased. Was it focusing? Growing more intense? *Gathering?* I could only keep my eyes on the mezzanine, put one foot ahead of the next and struggle against the escalator's infinite loop. Each step had to do "double-" or, perhaps more accurately, "quadruple-duty," what with the weight of the boots and the descending staircase—the tide against which I, ever the rapacious salmon, struggled. But if I persevered I would gain ground: I had to believe it! For it was faith that would propel me to victory. Faith and footsteps. Also my insatiable thirst for vengeance. Also the creepy hissing below.

The mall's second floor—my goal—was visible only as a levelling off of the top step, which flattened and vanished and was replaced again and again. Beyond it was the platform where I'd at last face my nemesis and literally "cut him down a size or two." Thus cowing his followers below. With one snip of my scissors I'd not only put an end to the ponytail's reign of terror but the infernal hissing and dancing of his minions and their false idol worship. In one fell swoop, or snip, all those copycat ponytails would droop as one. Or even fall to the food court floor in a great, shaggy cascade of defeat.

Another step. A backslide. Another step. And again the escalator diminished my progress. I advanced by degrees, to be sure—but they were marginal. Perhaps I mounted one stair for every ten paces, factoring in the continuous sweep downward that compromised each effort. So, imagining that there was perhaps a total of sixteen stairs on the escalator in a stationary position, that would require me to climb 160 steps, or the equivalent of ten flights!

But I would not be daunted. Below the hissing had reached a fever pitch, and I had to resist the image this conjured of the ponytails engaged in their hysterical aerobics, as rabid and feral as weasels. A fervour I knew all too well from my own former tongue-hair, how it had bucked against my teeth with heightening fervour until it tore itself free.

It was only a matter of time before Mr. Ponytail would appear and deliver some sort of stunning oratory or performance and perhaps unleash this deranged horde beyond the confines of the mall. God, I thought, struggling up another step, was *that* his scheme? Not just dominance of the mall, but of the whole town?

And why stop there? Why not consume the county, the region, the country—the *world*? He had to be stopped. And only I possessed the scissors to do so.

Upward I strained, progressing one step, back nine, and so on. I will spare further excruciating details, as things proceeded thusly (my labours, the hissing masses, various neurotic monologues playing through my thoughts, etc.) for a time. Eventually I was only two or three steps away from the landing—from the stage upon which our final duel would be fought, where I'd vanquish Ponytail and liberate the toadies below from his tyranny. My legs were barely operational. I made one step, slid back, another—another!

Finally I was a single stair away.

The mezzanine was cast in shadows. In the murk I could make out a few of the storefronts—Kookaburra's vitrine teeming with hideous sunflowers, like hydrocephalic, jaundiced heads lolling atop gangrenous necks. A putrid affair indeed. A few shops down the hall would be Dennis's former denim concern, the House of Blues—now a house of ill repute, per Mr. Ponytail's nefarious deceptions. Was he in there? Prepping himself for his showcase? With "mousse" and a brush? With the grinning spectre that Dennis had become?

Tragic, all of it.

I removed the scissors from my pocket and plunged forward another step.

The showdown was at hand.

I opened my scissors—flexed them, as it were. Ready to strike.

The hissing below rose up around me and seemed to thicken the air. I was jettisoned from the escalator onto the landing of the second floor. Luckily the weight of my boots held me fast, but still I reeled like a drunk before the abyss. It took a moment to steady myself before I could get my bearings and examine what faced me.

Well, you might have guessed it: hair.

The whole second floor was a great mat of the stuff, seething up the walls and all over the floor, seeming to produce a hiss and whisper of its own. I was sure all that hair I'd carried within me was braided in there too. Where was Mr. Ponytail? Nowhere in sight. Or perhaps everywhere. Perhaps this was him, incarnate— or, rather, in carpet.

Before I could turn to the escalator to "make myself scarcely there," its internal mechanism or engine produced a great metallic clunk and the thing paused and then began churning in reverse— now *ascending* at breakneck speed. One step on the thing and I'd be flung into the hair net. Which, meanwhile, was beginning to climb over my boots, strand by strand, in a kind of webbing. Its texture was not that of your average billowing ponytail, but coarse and bristly and sharp. The sort of hair you'd not want to run your fingers through but apparently which wanted to run through my fingers, and toes, and holes. And soul.

My god, was this how it would end? i.e., "it" being me?

Perhaps as it should be, I thought. I'd tried. I'd been defeated. I was nothing; Mr. Ponytail had shown me as much. Even my scissors were no match for this massive onslaught. A fine end: eaten by hair. What a way to go.

I hung my head and stood limply, waiting to be consumed. For the hair to haul me down and perhaps devour my body in some nutritional way, or else cart me off to its master's quarters to be repurposed as art. I could just imagine my various bits and pieces arrayed upon the walls of the mall—a great mural of me, with that signatory slash marking my remains as Ponytail's own.

But then, amid it all, I heard a voice.

A voice . . . calling my name?

I looked up.

K. Sohail!

Striding through the hair with a push mower—the manual sort whose blades require ambulation to chop and turn. And chop and turn they did! Carving right through the hair carpet with a shower of clippings spraying hither and thither and a trail of tiles plowed bare in her wake. A trail, mind you, that closed over as the hair resumed its form, but a trail that allowed her passage all the same.

And she was coming for me.

To my rescue? It certainly seemed so.

Quick, she cried. Loosen your boots!

So loosen them I did, bending down and prying open the buckles. A few errant or ambitious filaments went for me as I did, and I had to tear my hand away lest they ensnare me in that doubled-over compromising position, hand to foot like a petrified yogi. But then yes they were loose! And K. Sohail was nearly upon me. What now?

She arrived and—my, this was a surprise!—released her grip on the mower and hopped clean into my arms. What could I do but catch her?

For a moment I held her like that—like an adult-sized baby, or a sack of human flesh cleverly shaped into an actual human. We'd never touched before. She was warm. She smelled of bleach. Her breath felt nice on my neck. I liked her very much then.

But this was no time for feelings! The hair was making its ascent—up to the ankles of my loosened boots and rising.

Now step free! she commanded.

I was confused.

From the boots! Release yourself!

And then I understood.

One foot free—and my body began to tilt. The ghosts were churning. They were lifting us! What a scheme! How did K. Sohail know? Well, she was a caretaker. This is just what she did: took care. And she was taking care of me now as no one ever had. Amid these revelations I'd forgotten my instructions, and the hair was beginning to spill over the tops of my boots, to grip my flesh. K. Sohail yelled again: Do it! Now!

I yanked my other foot out of its boot.

Instantly we began to float.

The few stray bits that had tried to clutch my skin tore free. But as we drifted away from the hair all over the floor, we were angling toward the ceiling, which—my god, this was a bit much— also swarmed with hair.

Luckily K. Sohail knew just the thing. Paddling her hands, she manoeuvred us into the horizontal position of dream flight and steered us away. I did my best to help, though as I've mentioned I've never been much for swimming. Still, as a result of our combined efforts (surely I didn't hinder us) we floated out over the food court.

For a moment: stillness, hovering. And then I looked down.

Far below was a scene of absolute horror. The ponytails had . . . flipped. Each one was splayed over its owner's face, suctioned there like great spiders and seemingly pouring down into their open mouths. The hissing had been replaced by a gargling, desperate sound—but people were too tightly packed to escape. They could only bump blindly against one another as we lofted above and their own ponytails did them in.

Don't look, said K. Sohail, snatching my chin and pointing my face toward hers.

I thought for a moment she might kiss me. But she nudged my face further back, so I was looking straight up.

There, she said.

She intended to steer us to the skylight.

As we lifted, from the ring on her hip K. Sohail produced and readied a key.

Sunshine blazed just beyond that little window. I waited; the ghosts did their work. We floated. We rose. Shortly we were bumping up against the food court's high ceiling. I looked into K. Sohail's eyes. But she was focused on the lock: key in, turn. A click. She nodded at me again. I pushed the glass. Out it swung. In poured light and air. And then we were moving through.

WHAT'S YOUR NAME, I ASKED as we lifted into the daylight. Your good name. Your *actual* name.

She smiled. Leaned close to my ear. And, in a soft voice, told me. All five syllables.

Though of course I'd always known it.

And then we caught a breeze, soared a little higher, and were gone.

FINAL REPORT

Not submitted.

PASHA MALLA is the author of several works of poetry and fiction, including the story collection *The Withdrawal Method* and the novels *People Park* and *Fugue States*. His fiction has won the Danuta Gleed Literary Award, the Trillium Book Prize, an Arthur Ellis Award and several National Magazine awards. It has also been shortlisted for the Amazon.ca Best First Novel Award and the Commonwealth Prize, and longlisted for the Scotiabank Giller Prize and the International IMPAC Dublin Literary Award. Pasha Malla lives in Hamilton.